The Book of Sul

PATRICK D. CATLETT

This book is a work of fiction. Any resemblance to actual events or persons, living or dead, is entirely coincidental.

"The Book of Sul," by Patrick D. Catlett. ISBN 978-1-63868-120-5 (softcover).

Published 2023 by Virtualbookworm.com Publishing Inc., P.O. Box 9949, College Station, TX 77842, US.

Contents

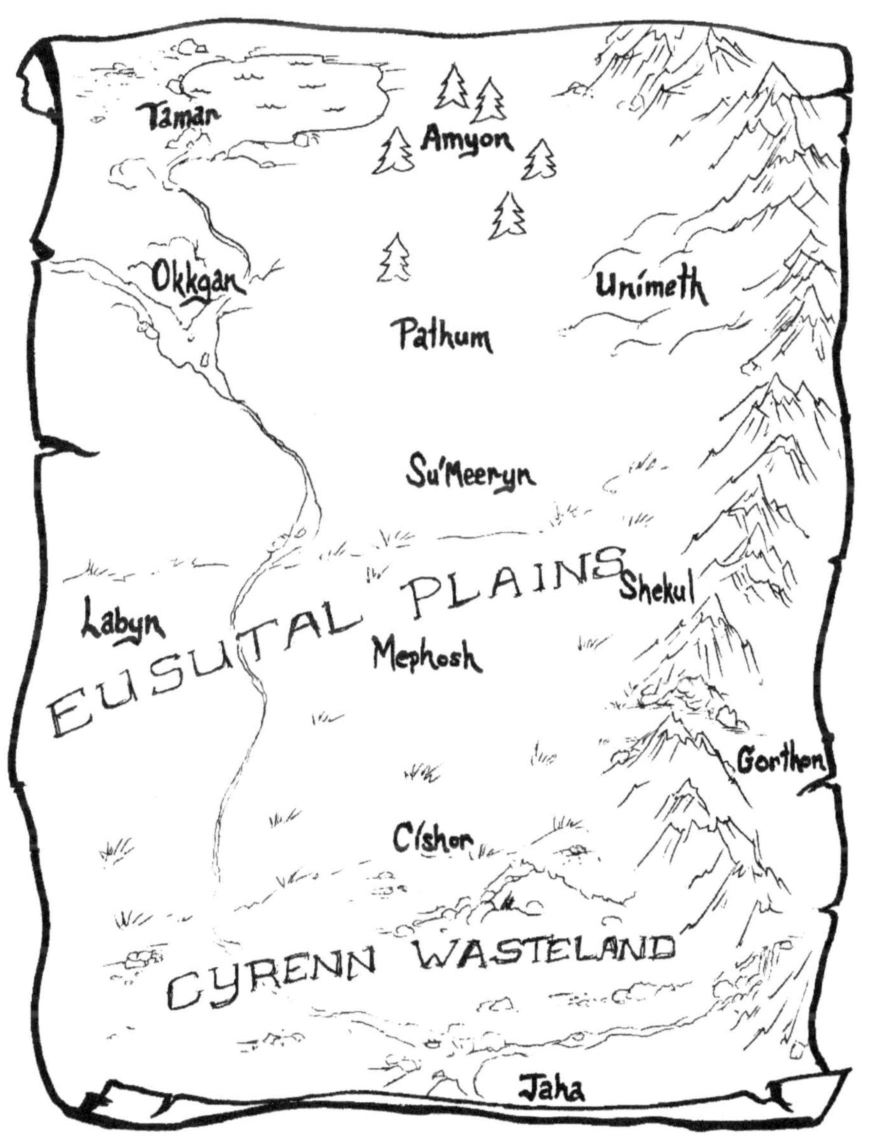
Tamar
Amyon
Okkgan
Unimeth
Pathum
Su'Meeryn
EUSUTAL PLAINS
Shekul
Labyn
Mephosh
Gorthon
C'shor
CYRENN WASTELAND
Jaha

Foreword

IN THE AGE THAT PRECEDED THE EVENTS in the Ring of Naar, small kingdoms still dotted the land, and the great empire of Xavsyn had not yet been established. Those kingdoms still bore the names that they would reclaim after being reformed once Xavsyn fell.

The land had experienced a generation of peace until a conflict arose between one of the smaller kingdoms, Su'Meeryn, and its more powerful neighbor, Mephosh. Many debated the cause of those hostilities. Some said it started from a trade disagreement. Others felt it was a religious dispute. While the cause remained a point of contention, the outcome was not. Su'Meeryn fell and became a vassal of Mephosh.

During this time, religion continued to be a dominant force amongst the nobility, and a strong priesthood in Mephosh exerted much power in the kingdom. The priests' authority was only superseded by the monarchy, but the common people found little use for the religion of the gods. However, they followed the sacraments when forced, due to fear of the priests.

Though Su'Meeryn remained a vassal, occasional skirmishes flared between the two cities, and that is where our story begins…

Prologue

"YOU DO REALIZE THAT YOU ARE GOING TO DIE tomorrow, don't you?" the inquisitor asked me, wearing a stoic expression.

"Yes," I replied with as little inflection in my voice as I could manage. How could I not know? The whole kingdom knew that I was to be executed at dusk the following day.

"You can still plead for mercy."

"Yes," I repeated, trying to match the flat tone from my previous reply.

"Do you want to die?"

Of course I did not want to die; who really wants to die? Life is better than death, but the weight of my past deeds weighed too heavily on me. I did not want to die, but I also did not care if I lived. I suppose that makes some sense. I looked out the small window, through the rusty bars, to the little blue sky I could see. My left hand absently brushed through my hair, and I immediately regretted the action as filth stuck to my fingers. I began picking out the grime, momentarily forgetting that I had a visitor until he coughed.

"I don't understand you." The man interrupted my brief musing. "There are many people who want to see you pardoned. Hasn't your time in this cell been punishment enough?"

A short chuckle escaped my cracked lips. I had not meant it to be audible. The time spent in this cell was certainly excruciating. The blazing heat of the days and the frigid nights. The meager portions of gruel that barely sustained me. The stink of my own excrement which was only removed prior to my visitors arriving. Yes, I suffered. But how did my suffering compare to all the others… my victims?

"No." I surprised myself that I had actually voiced the word. I had not meant to. It felt as if I was giving too much away. But what did it matter now? I then felt the all-too-familiar twinge of pain in my right shoulder, the constant reminder of my sins.

The inquisitor shook his head. "I guess I understand. I know your vile history, but what about all the good you did?"

I chuckled again, but this time I meant it to be audible. "You think you know, but you don't know anything."

He hesitated a bit, taken aback by my statement. "Then enlighten me."

There was no part of me that desired to tell this useless man my tale. I did not want anyone to know the full extent of my deeds. I wanted my story to die with me, thrown in the grave to be forgotten forever. But then I thought perhaps someone could learn from my mistakes. If that were the case, maybe my death would have some value.

"I will tell you my story on one condition. I want you to record this and pass it on."

The inquisitor looked at me for a moment, considering my request. I could tell he was not inclined to appease me, but he eventually acquiesced to my request.

The guard let him out of my cell. As I sat quietly, waiting, I again peered out that small window. My mortality weighed heavily on me, and a few tears escaped my eyes. I do not know if the tears were for myself or my victims, but I guess it did not matter. I wiped them away, and my internal debate ended when he reentered with a parchment. He sat down and tried to make himself as comfortable as possible on the hard, stone floor.

I then began to recount my tale.

chapter 1

I SAT AT THE GRINDING WHEEL, sharpening my sword. One might think it a strange place for a priest to find himself. However, this activity had become a common occurrence for me. I sometimes tried to lie to myself that I hated this, that I hated what I had become. However, it was not true. I relished it; I relished my role. I loved the kingdom, and I was fully devoted. I would do anything for Mephosh and her queen. The kingdom had made me a wealthy man. As a warrior and a priest, I was one of the most respected subjects in all the castle. And after the death of the king, the queen had come to rely on me probably more than anyone else in all of Mephosh. My importance to the kingdom could not be overstated.

A spark flew off the wheel and landed on my hand. "Careful," Gallun said from the wheel beside me as I stifled a curse under my breath. "How many did you kill?"

"I don't know. I lost count after ten," I answered with nonchalance.

Gallun's laugh revealed more than just some minor amusement. He knew me too well. Despite my occasional protests, he knew how I savored my role. We had schooled and trained together our entire lives. He was like a brother to me, and nobody knew me better. I turned and offered him a smile. At the time, I found his mirth regarding those who had fallen under my sword appealing. "When will they ever learn?" Gallun continued.

"If they haven't by now, it seems those dogs from Su'Meeryn never will."

Gallun stopped his wheel and examined his own sword. He flicked the blade with his fingernail and nodded his shaggy head in approval before he reached down, grabbed an oiled rag with his thick, scarred hands, and began polishing his weapon. "So, when do you go see the queen, Sul?"

I finished with my blade as well and also began to polish it. “After lunch,” I replied. Gallun sheathed his sword before turning back to me. He took a deep breath and let out a sigh. His hand went to his long, brown beard, and he scratched his chin. “Do you have a problem with that?”

“It must be nice to be in such a position. When will you be crowned the new king?”

After sheathing my own weapon, I pushed his shoulder a bit harder than just a playful gesture. The rumors regarding the queen and me had started not long after the king's death. Initially, I ignored them, but their persistence had begun to annoy me. The queen often sought my counsel, nothing more. At least she had not expressed any interest beyond that to me.

Besides, I had no desire to be king. My priestly duties kept me busy enough, not to mention when I went out to battle. Those were my passions. Being king would result in a completely new life. Power has its allure, but not enough to take those things away from me. I had no time for women. Perhaps a few years in the future when my body could no longer withstand the rigors of combat. But that time had not yet come.

“I’ll see you at temple tomorrow morning, Gallun,” was my only reply. And with that, I stood and headed towards the dining hall for my lunch. I wanted to arrive before the crowds so I would have time for meditation and prayers prior to meeting with the queen.

***

The royal chamber never failed to impress me whenever I entered. The bright marble floor was cleaned and polished daily. The sunlight beaming through the prismed glass windows created a sparkling display on the floor. The light reflected off the surface to the huge, jeweled chandeliers hanging from the darkly stained wood of the high ceiling. I did not know how the wood was kept unsoiled by the smoke residue of the candles. Obviously, servants had to clean the ceiling at night, but I never saw any sign of scaffolding. And I never once saw a scuff on the immaculately maintained floor.

Along the walls of the hall, under those huge windows, sat the benches for the crowds that gathered for various functions. The wood of the benches was stained to match the ceiling, and intricate carvings of animals and characters from the holy scriptures adorned the edges of each bench. However, the most impressive sight was the throne. The king’s dais sat on a pedestal of gold. The seat itself was made from marble, and precious gems and jewels adorned each side of the chair. Purple cushions covered the seat and back of the throne, along with the arm rests. The queen’s seat was to the left. It was smaller but also made of marble with matching cushions. Instead of precious stones, it was gilded in large hunks of silver with the occasional sliver of gold.

Since the king's death, the queen had taken to occupying the larger throne. Some in the court did not approve of this, but none dared to voice their displeasure to her. I had always found their disapproval petty. As our sole monarch, I figured she deserved the seat of highest honor, which is where I found her as I entered the hall. I strode across the marble floor, flanked by the royal guards dressed in polished, sparkling breast plates. Their gleaming helmets sported large purple plumes, and all their swords were unsheathed. They were required by tradition to always have weapons in hand while in the hall.

"My queen," I said as I reached the throne and lowered to one knee with arms stretched to my sides.

She gave me a warm smile and motioned for me to rise. As I did, she also stood from her seat. "Sul, always a pleasure to see you, my friend. Please come with me." She led me from the hall back towards her personal chambers, trailed by her two most trusted guards.

We sat across from each other at her small table, and I wondered how the rumors about the queen and me had started. While the years were creeping up on her, she was still a handsome woman. Gray had begun to encroach upon the black in her long, curly hair, and a few small wrinkles circled her almond eyes. If there were any additional blemishes on her skin, the cosmetics hid those.

It had always been assumed that the queen was barren, as she never bore the king children. But following his death, whispers began to surface that maybe the king was the problem. There was even a rumor that the king preferred young men and had never consummated the marriage, despite their many years together. I never saw any evidence of that, and I found it hard to believe. If it had been true and proven, we priests would have demanded his abdication, and he likely would have been imprisoned—if not worse.

Much like the talk about the queen and me, I never put much stock in those rumors. True, I would have been the first to vote for his removal if proven, but as long as they remained simply rumors, I did not care.

I guess the gossip was to be expected. Everyone had expected her to remarry, and she often summoned me to the hall. Perhaps a new king would give her the children the kingdom desperately desired, but I would certainly never be her choice. I am not a handsome man, and she could have her pick of all the eligible nobles in the kingdom. But with each passing year, remarriage seemed less and less likely, which frustrated the court. Who would succeed her as monarch? The queen seemed unconcerned with that matter. And soon, she would be past the age of childbearing. I often counseled her to consider marriage, but she always dismissed the suggestion. The last time I mentioned it, she displayed irritation, and I vowed never to bring the matter up again.

"How may I serve you, my queen?"

"Tell me about Su'Meeryn."

"Majesty?"

The queen leaned back in her chair with a sigh. "I don't always trust my advisors, Sul. Sometimes I wonder if they tell me what they think I want to hear. And I realize that not all of them are comfortable being subject to a woman. I know I don't have those concerns with you."

I once again found myself impressed with the queen's insightfulness and direct manner, unlike that of her husband. The king had been a dolt. "What can I tell you, my queen?"

"How many times do I have to ask for you to call me Lynna when we are alone?" Truthfully, I did not have an answer to that question, which, of course, was rhetorical. While I was certainly on friendly terms with the queen, I was under no illusions that she desired to be my friend. I always believed that her request was designed to increase my comfort with her and also my loyalty, which was not necessary. My eyes absently turned toward her guards and then back to her. "Fine," she said with a hint of playful annoyance, then continued. "I know we put down the insurrection, but why do they continue to rebel against me? I'm not so dreadful a queen, am I?"

She paused long enough that I realized she was now requesting an answer to her question, and I knew she wanted a truthful response. "You are very fair to all your subjects, Lynna, even those in Su'Meeryn." I did notice an almost imperceptible twitch at the corners of her mouth when I used her name. "Your taxes are fair, and you only ask for a reasonable number of men to join your army."

"Then what is it? Why do they continue to oppose me?"

I straightened in my seat to stretch my back a bit as I tried to loosen a knot developing under my shoulder blades. "As far as I can tell, I believe it has nothing to do with you. It seems it is a religious issue. I believe they do not want to be subjected to the faith."

The expressions that crossed Lynna's face were difficult to decipher. I thought I saw traces of both relief and agitation. The queen had always been very devout, unlike her husband, which was one of the reasons I was so loyal to her. The relief was that she was not the problem. However, if I was indeed correct, a religious dispute likely posed an even bigger dilemma. Hence her agitation.

"As always, Sul, I thank you for your time and honesty. I have much to ponder. You are excused, and I will call upon you when I have further issues to consider."

"My queen," I responded as I stood, but Lynna remained seated. I paused for a brief instance before turning to leave. What I saw before me was not the ruler of two kingdoms but a lonely and troubled woman. I wanted to offer some reassurance, but as I had already been dismissed, I had no choice but to promptly exit her chambers.

Chapter 2

GALLUN STOOD BESIDE ME, along with a score of other priests. Another of the chief priests read from the scriptures, and I stood and knelt as required. I raised my hands when it seemed appropriate, and a few tears streamed down my cheeks as emotions swelled. All in all, it was a normal service.

As usual, Gallun and I left the temple together after the ceremony concluded. My hands still dripped with the blood as it had been my honor to perform the sacrifice of the lamb this month, and we were required to not wipe them after completion. Many heads turned in our direction as we strolled down the streets of the city which encircled the castle. My bloody hands certainly created a spectacle, but our priestly robes alone would have caused a stir. The priests of Mephosh were highly revered. At least, that is what we told ourselves. Looking back, I believe what we experienced was not respect but fear.

Since this was the day of the lamb sacrifice, the temple was closed to the citizens of the kingdom. On these occasions, half of the priests were required to clean the sanctuary, but as Gallun and I had performed the task the previous month, we were excused for the day. With no additional priestly duties to perform, and no battles to head off to, we had the rest of the day free. That might sound pleasurable to some, but it was difficult to find activities for ourselves within the kingdom. Most people wanted no interaction with us priests. We were forbidden to enter a pub. Besides, I had no taste for ale, even if we were allowed to partake.

We could always participate in combat training, but I found little desire for that on this day. Gallun and I were both extremely skilled with all weapons, so sometimes training seemed tedious. Though secretly I desired to enter a brothel, the penalty for that was far more severe than going into a pub. Not only would I have been stripped of my robes, but

I would also lose my left hand. The only time Gallun or I partook of that sin was when we were at war. It was understood that if any other soldier found us with a prostitute, it would be ignored. Of course, everyone knew we were priests, but since we were risking our lives for the kingdom, we were allowed to indulge.

As we walked, Gallun looked up at the bright sky. "Still no rain," he muttered.

My gaze trailed his. "Yes, this is becoming very concerning. Crops are starting to wither."

"Perhaps the gods will respond to our pleas," he replied. "It was a moving service and an excellent sacrifice."

"Thank you," I said as we continued toward his house. On rare days such as this, we would spend our time at Gallun's home with his wife and young children.

***

We sat at the tiny table, sipping the wine that Gallun's wife had poured. "You treat us far better than we deserve, Juna," I commented as she sat beside her husband. She then offered me a rag to wipe my hands, but the blood had already dried.

"It's always a pleasure to have you over, Sul." She displayed a smile, but I saw no warmth in it. While I fancy myself a perceptive man, I could never quite tell if she truly held affection towards me or if her affability was manufactured. There were times I felt she did care for me, but other times I believed she was simply putting on a façade. Being one of the priests, I often ran into this dichotomy. More often than not, I could tell the difference. However, Juna remained a mystery. On a number of occasions, I thought of quizzing Gallun on the subject, but I did not want to put him ill at ease. As he was my only true friend, I did not want to risk anything that might jeopardize that. In actuality, her inner feelings were of no consequence. They changed nothing regarding my friendship with her husband. "Tell me about Su'Meeryn," she continued. "My husband seems always to want to keep me in the dark after you two go off to war."

I glanced at my friend for a sign that he might want me to remain silent, but he seemed to have ignored her comment as he took a long sip from his mug. "Not much to tell," I replied. "They continue to resist maintaining proper worship practices. Lynna is concerned that this might cause them to want to break away from her rule."

"I'm well aware of that," she chided me. "What I want to hear about is what you did there. Gallun tells me nothing."

"Well…" I stammered for a moment. It was not often I felt I did not have the upper hand in a conversation, but Juna's questioning on the subject brought that about. All the educated in Mephosh knew what was occurring in Su'Meeryn, but it was not my place to enlighten Juna any further if Gallun chose not to. We had killed a number of soldiers to put down the small uprising. Gallun was not generally one to shy away from boasting regarding those we had killed, but perhaps he wanted to spare Juna from seeing him that way. I did not know, and it was not any of my business. After regaining my composure, I continued, "if you want details regarding our time there, I suggest you ask your husband. I will not go against his wishes in this matter."

"You men, do you think I am too frail to hear of your deeds?"

"Ask Gallun," was my only response.

"I'm tired of these secrets from you two. I can certainly—"

"Enough woman!" Gallun interrupted as he slammed his mug to the table. "You brought us the wine, now leave us!"

Juna glared at her husband and then looked to me. I attempted to remain expressionless, but I did not know if I had succeeded. Gallun's temper was well known, and I figured Juna was attempting to get me to confess of our trip to the Su'Meeryn brothel following the battle. If he had not mentioned it to her, I certainly was not going to. Juna's face turned red as her gaze shot back to Gallun. I thought she was going to respond, but she just rose and stomped away from the table.

"You are fortunate that you never married," Gallun quipped, though he certainly did not mean it. He had been harassing me for years to take a wife, and I knew he loved Juna. But as priests, it was not often that we were questioned or not treated with reverence. Therefore, it was frustrating to him on the rare occasions when he felt disrespected.

"Where are the children?" I asked, purposely changing the subject.

Gallun looked down at his mug, and I could see his displeasure that most of the remaining contents had spilled out when he had slammed it down. The wine flask remained on the counter, and he clearly did not want to stand to retrieve it. So he swallowed what remained, then wiped his mouth. "They are at their lessons."

Outside of the noble class, only priests' children were eligible for schooling. All other male children learned the trades of their fathers, while the daughters learned from their mothers. If a child was an orphan…well, those were destined to be barely above that of a slave. They would learn a menial trade in the orphanage with little hope of ever improving their lot.

I nodded and also finished my wine. We then chatted about a number of rumors regarding the nobles of Mephosh. Eventually, Juna rejoined us, the outburst between the two forgotten. As the day progressed, Juna turned her attention to preparing the evening meal. When his children arrived home, Gallun required a review of their lessons. They had learned to read some time ago, so most of their lessons were regarding the scriptures. However, today had been spent reviewing the history of Mephosh. I found this extremely satisfying, as our kingdom's past was of huge interest to me. The only topic I found of surpassing import was religion. I quizzed them for a time and was impressed with their answers.

When we were done, the children ate a quick meal, then went off to their room, leaving the three of us to enjoy more wine. "Perhaps this drought is due to the heretics in Su'Meeryn," Juna mused. "I'm sure that the gods are not pleased."

"An astute observation," responded Gallun before leaning over and kissing her cheek. She smiled brightly at the unusual show of affection, but I figured it had more to do with the wine than anything else.

As expected, I was invited to stay for dinner. I gladly accepted. The conversation remained pleasant throughout the evening. Afterward, we enjoyed a few more mugs of wine. As I stood, Juna gently grabbed my cloak and gazed at me with an expression of sorrowful affection. The wine was clearly affecting her as well. "We still need to find you a woman, Sul. I ran into Kieran at the market today; she still does not have a man."

Kieran was a beautiful woman who had been married to one of the minor nobles of Mephosh. They had two children, but both died as infants. Her husband had succumbed to a fever about a year ago. After that, for some reason, she started working in the armory with Wander, the head armorer.

"I appreciate your concern, my friends, but I am happy with my life as it is." With that, I excused myself. I wanted to return home before the hour became too late. As an early riser, I did not want to become too groggy before I could finish my evening prayers.

After reaching my home, I spread my prayer blanket on the ground, knelt down, and recited all the required petitions, along with a few extra for rain. Once completed, I moved to light a candle so I could complete my nightly readings. Prior to striking the flint, I felt exhaustion creep up, likely due to all the wine. I was always annoyed with myself when I did not complete my daily routines, but I knew I would not be able to remain awake. I decided to let sleep overtake me so I would be ready for the morning.

***

The following days flowed by without incident. I worked in the temple, receiving sacrifices from the Mephosh citizens. As one of the upper echelons in the priesthood (unlike Gallun), I also sat on the priestly court. We heard disputes on religious matters and interpreted scriptures for worshippers when they had questions. As the final arbiters of religion, all our rulings were final; not even the queen could question them. The power was exhilarating, but I always tried my best not to show my pleasure and to follow the will of the gods. Many of my evenings were spent arms training with Gallun, but usually, most of those times involved teaching the less-skilled warriors.

And then, unfortunately, several weeks later, word came back of further unrest in Su'Meeryn. I say 'unfortunately,' but I really do not mean that. I knew Gallun and I would be summoned to accompany the expedition to crush the insurrection, and I was eager to meet the challenge. It had been too long since I had entered combat. Nothing gave me more pleasure than leveling justice upon heretics, and perhaps this justice would appease the gods' anger.

The lack of rain was becoming an increasing problem. Many of our crops had perished, and a couple of the wells had run dry. There remained enough water for the citizens and our livestock to drink, but for how long? The queen's concerns multiplied with each dry day, and the extra sacrifices offered still had not caused the gods to relent.

The morning could not arrive soon enough.

Chapter 3

As we left the outskirts of Mephosh, I rode at the head of the column with Gallun beside me. While I was technically not in command of the soldiers, everyone deferred to me as a chief priest. My commanders would never question me on the battlefield. Even Gallun would refrain from his playful jabs when we were out on a mission.

While I did love my priestly duties, and I would not have traded them for anything, this is what I relished: heading off to battle to put heretics in their place. There was no greater calling.

The route north towards Su'Meeryn was an easy ride through the Eusutal Plains. With good weather, it took about two days. Since our horses would not need rest, we rode straight to Su'Meeryn without a break. As we approached, we spotted a small contingent of riders heading toward us, and we drew our weapons. I slowed my steed somewhat; I wanted to survey the situation prior to making contact.

As we got closer, I realized there were only about a half-dozen men confronting us. I sheathed my blade, and I heard the same from the warriors trailing me. A quick glance at Gallun showed that his sword remained in his hand. That was fine with me. I did not want to appear provocative, but I supposed it was good that Gallun kept himself ready. The riders from Su'Meeryn stopped not far from us, and the leader of their group raised his hand in either greeting or deference. I did not care which. I continued forward with Gallun and a number of soldiers trailing.

"Greetings," the leader said. "Our scouts reported your passage, and I wanted to ride out to welcome you to our land."

I gazed at the man. I did not immediately reply, as I wanted to make him feel uncomfortable by my pause. "Do you know why we are here?"

"We do not, but our brothers from Mephosh are always most welcome." I examined the man's expression and could tell that he was lying. Why would we be welcome after our prior visit?

"I suggest that you move your horses and allow us to pass," I continued as I placed my hand on the hilt of my sword.

"Please sir, there is no need for threats. King Teyon welcomes you to Su'Meeryn. He wants to avoid an unfortunate outcome, such as the last time, and he is anxious to greet you."

I leaned forward on my horse with my hand still resting on the sword hilt. "There is no king in Su'Meeryn," I hissed. "By her benevolence, Queen Lynna allows Teyon to remain as regent. He is not king."

The man's pretense of ease was disintegrating; he stammered for a moment before answering. "Of course, my apologies. I did not mean any disrespect to your queen. I—"

"Our queen," I corrected as I sat back in my saddle.

"Of course, sir," he responded as his face started to flush, and I could see the conflict within him as he attempted to hide his growing anger. "Our queen. Now, if you would permit me, I will escort you to Teyon."

"Lead the way."

***

The individual we were led to, sitting before me, whom Gallun and I had met on our prior visit to Su'Meeryn, was a beaten man. That last time had concluded with much violence, and I fully expected this trip to end the same. But to be fair to Teyon, I did not believe he was the cause of any of the insurrections. He knew he would pay the ultimate price if any of the rebellions were traced back to him, and clearly, he was happy that he at least maintained some semblance of power after Mephosh had conquered Su'Meeryn. My counsel to Lynna was against letting him live, but she had wanted to appear merciful to the Su'Meeryn citizens. However, her patience was starting to run short.

"It is Sul, correct?" Teyon stated as I strode through what was once the royal chamber with Gallun beside me. About a dozen soldiers trailed after us. Dust and dirt fell from our weathered bodies amidst the hall stripped of the precious jewels that had once adorned it. Only the wooden floor and chairs remained, so who cared about some dirt that fell here or there?

"Teyon," I acknowledged, and I spotted a trace of annoyance he failed to camouflage as I did not use a title. "Why are we here again? Your queen is not pleased."

"Your visit was not requested."

I laughed at his comment. Was he playing me for a fool, or did he truly not know what was happening in his former kingdom? I took a few more steps closer to where he sat, where the throne of Su'Meeryn once rested. "If you wish to remain regent, you are required to carry out Queen Lynna's commands. She is very displeased to be informed that your religious folk continue to stray from orthodoxy. Why do you allow this to happen?"

"You are putting me in an extremely difficult position, Sul. Su'Meeryn has acted as a loyal subject to Mephosh. We have no desire to see troops from your land in our streets, and yes, I do realize that would incur additional taxes to compensate the queen. But what would you have me do?"

"Stop them," Gallun interjected.

"That is easy to say, but how do you propose I accomplish that? Kill them?"

"Not the worst idea," Gallun continued.

Teyon took a breath to contain himself. "You want me to kill my own citizens? Don't you realize that would cause even more problems?"

"And what of this drought?" I asked.

"What of it?"

"The gods clearly are unhappy with the dealings in Su'Meeryn," Gallun stated. "We can't have a fringe group of heretics responsible for such suffering."

"Surely you can't blame the drought on Su'Meeryn," spat Teyon.

"The rains stopped following the first upheaval," I pointed out. "And let me remind you, these are not your citizens."

Teyon no longer attempted to suppress his anger. "Fine," he hissed. "Correct my language all you want, but that does not change the fact that more violence will cause even more problems than you have right now."

"Your point is taken," I responded, ignoring his irritation, which was irrelevant to me. The only thing that mattered was that he carried out his role. If we wanted Teyon to remain effective as regent, the people of Su'Meeryn needed to trust him. All the more reason I still felt he should have been killed and a new regent established, but Lynna had made it clear that she would entertain no further discussion regarding the matter. "You will have your men take us to the agitators, and once again, we will resolve the situation for you. However, I warn you, this will be the last time. If these upheavals continue, the response towards you and all of Su'Meeryn will be far more severe."

"Threats are unnecessary, Sul."

"I disagree. They appear to be extremely necessary." I immediately turned and led Gallun and the rest of our warriors from the hall.

***

The man, Jaleph, who had met us on the outskirts of Su'Meeryn, and brought us to Teyon, guided us through the streets of the village. He was a lean, tall man but very muscular. Bright blue eyes shone from his chiseled face. Short brown hair barely reached the nape of his neck, and he carried an air of unwavering confidence. Gallun had tried to engage him in some conversation as we headed toward our confrontation, but Jaleph responded in only monosyllabic words. It was a bit out-of-character for Gallun to act friendly towards a perceived enemy, but I guessed he was becoming bored with the whole situation. That seemed odd to me, as I knew what awaited us, and Gallun did too. He probably felt that some conversation would pass the time prior to the inevitable violence.

"We will be outside the temple shortly," Jaleph stated. "I hope you will do everything in your power to end this peacefully."

"It did not end peacefully the last time we were here," Gallun pointed out. "What makes you think that is a possibility now?"

"Just hope," answered Jaleph quietly. "I pray you try."

"We will do what we need to do. I suggest your soldiers do the same once we are gone," I stated sharply.

Jaleph turned to me. His mouth opened for a moment, but then he closed it again and continued in silence. After the brief journey, we turned a corner and stood before the temple. I signaled, and the warriors that had been following drew their weapons and spread out in the street beside me. A score of worshippers were knelt on the ground in prayer. When they heard us, they all stood, and one man strode forward. "You are Sul. I remember you from the last time."

"I am pleased you remember me, but I cannot say the same of you."

"Why are you here?"

"You know why we are here," Gallun interjected. "I thought we made ourselves very clear during our prior visit. Your queen will not tolerate heretics in her realm."

"We are not heretics."

"You do not worship the gods," I pointed out. "That is the definition of heresy. You are an affront to them, and your heresy has brought on this drought."

"Worshipping the creator is not heresy, and our actions are not the cause of the lack of rain. Perhaps it is the other way around."

I glared at the man as I slowly drew my sword. I did not know how often we would be forced into the same conversation with these maggots. "As you are aware, we are all part of one realm, and the queen will not tolerate divergent religions. You will follow the true path and worship the gods. I will not continue to repeat myself. All of you must disperse, now, and your temple will be cleared of any apostasy."

"We will not."

I felt my pulse quickening as it was clear this confrontation would end only one way. "Jaleph, order these *worshippers* to disperse," I commanded.

"We will not," the man repeated.

Gallun raised his sword and said, "Last chance."

The man stood defiantly before us and did not respond further. He then turned and gestured to the other clerics, and they all returned to their knees and continued with their futile gibbering.

"So be it," I muttered as my sword struck the side of the man's head. Blood erupted as I felt his skull crack from my blow. The man's body crumpled before me, and I heard a cry of glee escape from Gallun. He pounced at the nearest worshipper and drove his sword through the man's neck. A crimson explosion drenched Gallun, but he did not appear to notice. He merely turned to his next victim. The man's eyes were closed as Gallun stood above. The smile on Gallun's face started to fade as his sword pierced the man's heart. His pleasure in this slaughter was spoiled by the lack of opposition.

With that, the violence abruptly ended. As we had been met with no resistance, my warriors made quick work of all the clerics. I glanced about. The unarmed bodies were strewn everywhere, with blood still flowing in all directions. I did not feel pleasure at the sight of death, but I also did not feel remorse. Choices resulted in consequences, and these men had made their choice.

"I hope you will control your people now," I said to Jaleph as he just stared ahead, his mouth agape, while I wiped off my blade with the cloak of one of the dead heretics. "This would not have been necessary if you and Teyon had done your jobs."

Jaleph turned to me, and I saw the disdain on his face. I could tell he wanted to answer, but again, he restrained himself. He must have figured there was no point. Whatever he might say would change nothing. "My men will need a diversion after all this before we return to Mephosh." Jaleph nodded as he motioned for the soldiers to follow him. I fell in line but had decided I would not partake in the carnal activities. As we exited the area, frightened onlookers began to remove the bodies. I stopped for a moment to watch, but I quickly caught up to Jaleph and my men. I did not think I was in any danger, but perhaps someone might do something stupid if I remained there by myself.

I ordered Jaleph to take me back to the hall. I would spend my time alone in prayers until Gallun and the others were done with the brothels.

***

The ride back to Mephosh was fairly quiet. Gallun had wanted to talk about his *activities,* but I was not in the mood. I was not bothered by the killings. The men were heretics and had received righteous justice. However, I was concerned about what might happen next. There already had been two episodes of violence between Mephosh and Su'Meeryn in a relatively short timeframe. I did not respect Teyon, but I was worried he might take a drastic step in response to this episode.

Gallun had scoffed that thought away. He said Teyon was a coward and cared more about maintaining his position as regent than seeking retribution. I understood Gallun's point, but I was not convinced. Teyon had once been the king of Su'Meeryn. Might this push him over the edge? And this man Jaleph concerned me. I did not like the look of him, but I figured we would find out soon enough. Plus, despite our actions to please them, the gods still refused to relent and provide rain.

Chapter 4

I ONCE AGAIN FOUND MYSELF in Queen Lynna's chambers. She was pondering my description of the recent events, but that seemed unnecessary to me. We had both known how my mission would likely end, so I found it somewhat disconcerting that she had not prepared herself for this actuality. "What do you suppose will happen next?" she asked.

"Unclear," I responded. "I think Teyon is a weak man. He is comfortable as regent, but he remembers what it was like to be king. I'm sure he would prefer that the taxes filled his coffers rather than yours. The slaughter of those priests will certainly have ramifications, and I don't know how strong he will be in squashing any additional uprisings or dissent. Might he actually encourage additional strife?" I paused for a moment. "Maybe Teyon isn't the one we should worry about. That Jaleph does concern me. I sensed a strength in him."

"Who?"

"Oh, my apologies. Jaleph was the man who met us on the outskirts of Su'Meeryn, and he was the one who took us to the temple. He could be a problem if Teyon allows it."

"I'm not worried about one man," Lynna commented, waving her hand dismissively. "Teyon will fall in line. And before you remind me, I know you always wanted him killed. I still think he is more valuable to us alive."

"I'm not sure I concur, my queen."

"If you are concerned about tension between Su'Meeryn and Mephosh, wouldn't killing him at this time only increase those tensions?"

"You may be right," I had to agree.

"Should we send more troops there now?"

I had to think about her question for a moment, and I wondered why I had not anticipated it. "That might be a good idea, but you would have to increase taxes even more to send and sustain a substantial presence."

"That is true, and it will cause further consternation in Su'Meeryn. But they need to know there are ramifications for their disobedience."

"You could tell them that the increased troops and taxes are temporary until they finally put an end to the heretics. That would likely cause some internal strife within Su'Meeryn. Some of their citizens might then see the heretics as the problem."

The queen smiled at my comment, and I saw the look of solidified determination cross her face. She took a sip from the silver goblet beside her before she continued, "Agreed. I will make arrangements. As always, I thank you, Sul, for your wise counsel. You may return to the temple."

***

My religious obligations were always a pleasure. I enjoyed returning to my worship duties following the recent events in Su'Meeryn. Focusing on the gods took my mind away from temporal distractions and concerns. I spent more time than normal praying to the gods of the harvest as I begged them for rain. It was satisfying to focus strictly on the divine and put all the strife of this world to the side, at least for the moment.

After completing my prayers and rituals, along with administering sacraments for the citizens, I was able to spend some time with Gallun, preparing the temple for the following day's activities.

"How is the training of your children coming?" I asked my friend.

Gallun set down the candelabra he'd been polishing. "They are doing well. I heard that you saw Lynna again this morning."

I chaffed a bit at the informality with which he referred to our monarch, though this was not the first time he called her by name when we were alone. "Yes, she wanted to discuss what happened in Su'Meeryn and what steps to take next." I inspected the basin I had been cleaning, then set it down on a shelf.

"And?"

"And she is going to send troops there until Teyon resolves this heretic issue."

"Smart," Gallun replied, dusting off the book of scriptures. "That should put pressure on them from their own people. I suppose she will have to increase their taxes, which will anger them even more."

"Exactly. Perhaps the people of Su'Meeryn will solve their own problem for us." I inspected the room and decided that we had completed all our tasks for the temple to be ready the following day. "We've done enough here. Let's head over to the courtyard for some sparring. While this plan will hopefully solve the problem, we should make sure we are fully prepared if not."

Gallun slapped me on the back and led the way from the temple. "Very good, my friend. It will be nice to get sweaty before returning home. Juna loves me when I'm damp and smelly," he said with a wry grin.

As always, as we walked through the city of Mephosh, all the people we encountered did their best to avoid us. While the citizens honored the priesthood, they did not want to interact with us. They felt no good would come from that. If they said the wrong thing or acted the wrong way, we might order more penance then they were accustomed too. And they were probably correct. I relished finding flaws with the masses, and Gallun felt the same way. So it was very uncommon for us priests to have friends amongst the citizens or even the nobility. The only time a layman might push for interaction with us was if a priest had made it known he was seeking a wife. It was viewed as a coup if a man managed to marry off a daughter to one of us.

We jostled with each other as we made our way through the streets, which caused even more questioning eyes than normal. When we reached the training courtyard, we changed out of our priestly robes and went to the armory to get our wooden weapons.

When we reached the building, we were greeted by the head armorer, a burly dark-skinned man from Gorthon named Wander. He had worked in the armory for many years and was normally very quiet. Wander had always been pleasant. However, as of late, his attitude toward me seemed to exhibit a semblance of hostility.

"How may I help you, gentleman?" he asked with a tone of clearly feigned joviality.

Gallun recognized the thinly veiled adversarial tone, as did I. "Blunt weapons," he commanded with a scowl.

Wander portrayed no hint of aggravation at the stern response from my friend. He signaled to the back, and Kieran emerged from the shadows with our weapons. She was slightly younger than Gallun and me but still quite beautiful. Her red hair cascaded halfway down her back like lava. Her smooth, creamy skin displayed no blemishes, even with no visible sign of cosmetics. Under her petite nose, full lips matched the color of her hair. She wore a long, baggy cloak that hid what I knew to be a very appealing body.

It was strange for a woman to work in the armory, but no one questioned her following the death of her husband. As she handed the items to Wander, she offered Gallun and me a smile, which did not hide the cold disdain in her eyes. I was not surprised to see this expression directed at me, but it was a little odd toward Gallun, since Kieran and Juna had started to become friends.

"Here you are, gentlemen," Wander said matter-of-factly, holding the weapons out to us.

Gallun snatched them from the dark, callused hands and spun away. "What's his problem?" he asked as we strode through the courtyard.

"I don't know. I have noticed he's been rather short with me of late."

"Well, he'd better watch himself."

I nodded as we took position in the courtyard. We bowed to each other before taking our combat stances. Gallun was the first to swing, but I easily deflected the strike. Of course, it was not designed to actually hit me. He was only getting the match started. We traded blows for a bit, and, surprisingly, he was the first to contact flesh. While Gallun was an extremely skilled fighter, it was well-known throughout Mephosh that I was the strongest warrior in the land.

Gallun smiled broadly as he continued to press his assault. He kept me on the defensive, but I stopped his weapon from finding my body again. I then tried to press my own attack, only to feel the wood strike my left shoulder. Frustration set in, and I pushed further, which only resulted in Gallun connecting again.

We sparred for about an hour, and while I did manage to get some blows past him, Gallun clearly had the better of me that day. When we were finished, we headed to his house, and he was beaming the whole way.

We entered his home late in the afternoon, and Gallun offered me a rag to wipe off any lingering sweat from my body as he changed into fresh clothes. Juna was busy in the kitchen but offered me a goblet of wine, which I gratefully accepted. She advised me that the children would not be home until later in the evening, which was disappointing. As I had no children of my own, I always enjoyed their presence. She said that, after finishing their lessons, they would be spending time in the stables. Gallun had seen to it that they were learning about all the various jobs within the kingdom. He certainly did not expect them to enter any of those vocations, but he wanted them to have full knowledge of all the workings of Mephosh, even the insignificant ones.

After emerging from his room, Gallun poured wine for himself while Juna continued with her meal preparations. "Do you have your purse?" he asked me while placing his mug on the table. When I nodded, he went over to the counter to grab a set of dice. Juna did not approve of our gambling, and I heard her huff under her breath as I glanced at Gallun. He certainly heard her as well, but he ignored the sound. I did not blame her, as gambling was a forbidden activity, but we only wagered between ourselves when we were at one of our homes. I had rationalized that it was more for entertainment than truly betting, so we had made the decision not to worry about it. Wine and brothels were also forbidden to priests, but we partook of those as well—wine far more often than prostitutes.

We rolled the dice for a short while until the meal was ready. I was again annoyed that Gallun was getting the better of me in the game, but I had taken far more of his money over the years than he had mine. Before Gallun could roll again, Juna placed the cooked slices of meat on the table along with some carrots and nuts. She snatched the dice from his hand and placed them back on the shelf before joining us for the meal.

She asked us about our day, but we did not have much to report. We mentioned that we had seen Kieran at the armory, and, as usual, Juna chided me about when I was going to take a wife. She reminded me that Kieran remained unattached. I thanked her for her concern regarding my wellbeing and told her I would certainly let her pick out a wife for me if I ever decided to marry.

"What do you think about Wander?" Gallun asked, saving me from further prodding regarding my marital status.

"Who is Wander?" Juna replied with a grin that showed her understanding it was time to discuss a different topic.

"He is the master at the armory," I answered.

"Oh, yes. Kieran has mentioned him," she continued. "What happened?"

"Nothing actually happened. He was simply rather short with us when your husband and I came for our sparring weapons."

"Not too smart to anger a couple of priests," Juna pointed out, pleased with her observation.

"No, it's not," Gallun concurred. "That's what troubles me."

"What have you two been hearing at the temple?"

I looked at her quizzically. "What do you mean?"

"This thing with Wander got me thinking. I've overheard some whispers when I've been to the market recently."

"Whispers?" asked Gallun. "Whispers of what?"

"Well, your last mission was to quell some heretics of the gods in Su'Meeryn, right? Every now and then, it seems someone might be secretly talking of a new cult here in Mephosh."

"What cult?" I asked, sitting up a little straighter.

"Yes, what are you talking about, woman? And why am I just hearing about this now?" The anger was clearly growing in Gallun, and I placed my hand on his wrist to calm him down.

Juna stammered briefly. "It's just… I didn't think anything of it at first. You know how things are at the market. Rumors and gossip fly, but most amount to nothing. I had dismissed it as simply that, even after you had returned from Su'Meeryn. You said that the heretics worshipped only one god, but now that you mention the armory, one of the rumors said something about maybe meeting there." When she finished, I saw the apprehension on her face. She clearly did not know how Gallun was going to react.

"You did well, Juna," I responded before my friend could say anything. "We will look into this tomorrow."

She gave me a grateful smile as she rose to clear the table and poured us each more wine. "Do you think this has something to do with the lack of rain?" she continued. "These apostates must be angering the gods."

"Very possible," I replied. She then brought the dice back and left us to our game.

"We will need to see Nikkeudm in the morning," I said as I threw the first roll.

***

Nikkeudm was the leader of the priesthood. Outside of Lynna, he was the only person in the kingdom more powerful than me. He was an ancient and weathered man. The stories held that when he was younger, his warrior skills had far surpassed mine. I always wondered about those tales, but I did not necessarily doubt them. He had once been very tall, but age had not been kind to him. His many years had hunched him over. A myriad of scars covered his body, and what had once been muscle had turned into fat that flapped whenever he moved, much like the flags that covered the castle walls. Yet despite the deterioration of his body, his mind remained sharp.

He motioned for us to sit as we entered his private study. "How may I assist two of my favorite clerics?" he asked in his raspy voice. His still-sharp blue eyes darted between the two of us. It was not often the head of our order had visitors. We all knew our roles, and we did not need any direction from our leader. He had become too feeble to perform priestly duties himself, so he spent most of his time alone in his study.

"I assume that someone has briefed you about our mission to Su'Meeryn," I began, and Nikkeudm nodded. "We have heard a troubling rumor that a cult might be forming here in Mephosh as well. We don't know if it is related to the one in Su'Meeryn, but the timing might not be coincidental. And we have reason to believe that Wander may be connected to it. I'd like to take a contingent of priests to search the armory."

"I see," the old priest said. "Well, we certainly do not want any cults taking root in Mephosh. We must do all we can to appease the gods. Hopefully, they will relent soon and end this damnable drought. I assume that you both have duties today. I will assemble a list and notify the men that they will be under your command first thing in the morning. If you do find evidence of heretics here, I know that you will resolve the situation."

"Of course, sir," I said with a large smile.

***

An amber hue spread in the early morning sky as Gallun and I made our way toward the armory, with a score of priests trailing us. We all had swords sheathed at our sides and clubs in our hands. When we reached the armory, we saw no movement and no lights in the building. If there was cultic activity happening there, we had no idea what days they would take place. It would have to be either early morning or late in the evening, as certainly, blasphemous activities would not occur during the day hours.

The men and I squatted down in a small grove of trees beside the armory to keep an eye on the door. We waited a bit as I figured we should give it some time to see if anyone came prior to searching the building. As the sun began to rise, my plan was rewarded as we spotted the unmistakable frame of Wander approach. For the man just to be doing his armory duties, there was no reason for him to arrive so early. Gallun grunted as he began to rise, but I grabbed his arm to restrain him. He shot me an angry look as I pulled him back to a seated position. "Wait," I whispered. "Let's see if others come."

Gallun nodded his assent, and his attention returned to the armory. It did not take long for my restraint to pay off as about a half dozen other individuals began to arrive and enter the building. I signaled for my group to wait a little longer in case others showed up. After a short while, with the lights now burning in the building and no more movement outside, I rose from behind my tree and strode quietly to the door. I did not need to look back to know that the others followed.

I stood for a moment with my club in hand, giving the other priests time to situate themselves. I told myself not to overreact as I did not know what we would find once we entered. We were still operating solely on rumors, and I did not want to accuse an innocent man. So, rather than barging through the door, I gently opened it and stepped over the threshold.

Unfortunately, the scene was what we had all expected. Wander and the others knelt in a circle, in prayer, with a candle before them. A quick glance showed no idols or any other icons of the gods. Performing a religious service with no priest present was bad enough, but a cultic service was an abomination. "What is the meaning of this?" I bellowed.

The heretics jumped off the ground at the sound of my voice. Besides Wander, I recognized one additional person. Kieran stood up next to the large, dark man. Fear shone in their eyes, so I knew the rumors were in fact true. Dread was palpable on all of them except Wander. He just glared at me. It was not a glare of fear or anger but a glare of resolve. "Why are you here?" he asked.

"We don't need to answer that," Gallun stated. "You need to answer Sul."

"Sir," one of the others stammered. "We aren't hurting anybody."

"Not hurting anybody? The lack of rain tells a different tale. Now, I ask again, what is going on here?" I continued my questioning as I felt my tolerance about to evaporate.

Wander looked at each of the others in turn, an unspoken order not to respond. He folded his hands, and his lips began to move in silent prayer. Then Kieran and the others followed his example. I gestured to one of my other priests. He came up to Wander and struck him in the midsection with his club. Wander fell to his knees with a loud grunt while the other heretics began to cry.

"I am not going to repeat myself," I hissed. "What is going on here?"

"We are praying to the creator," one of the others blurted out.

My head turned as I studied each of these misguided worshippers. "I see. So the filth from Su'Meeryn has infected Mephosh now? You all know that heresy is illegal in Her Majesty's kingdom. And now you will pay the price."

I raised my club and smashed a hard blow against the chest of the man who had responded to me. I heard the sickening thud and the sound of bones cracking. He cried out in pain as his other hand grasped at his injury. My next blow struck his knee, and he crumpled to the ground. My booted foot kicked his face, and blood burst from his nose. He fell face-first to the floor, and I continued to kick his back and legs. He whimpered for mercy as blood continued to pool around him.

Gallun and the other priests were also administering ecclesiastical justice. Of the seven heretics in the room, three were women, but I could not let them be spared. They were equally guilty and deserved the same punishment. One of the other priests had become a bit overzealous with clubbing blows to the torso of a whimpering heretic before I finally stopped him.

The room was awash with a crimson stain, and the cries of pain had subsided as all the apostates were now unconscious. I did a quick inspection of myself, and I was not splattered with much blood. I could not say the same of the others. "Have them taken to the dungeons," I ordered. "We will question them when they are able to speak. We need to know if there are others in Mephosh of similar beliefs. Once we are done with the questioning, display them in the courtyard. If any of them do not survive, put their bodies on exhibit immediately. I will not have this travesty infiltrate our great kingdom any further."

***

Later that day, after being informed that Wander was awake and able to speak, I made my way to the dungeons. He had displayed an air of leadership in the group, so he was probably the best person to question.

When I entered his cell, I found him sitting quietly on a stool with his left eye closed. The bruising was hard to see on his dark skin in that low light, but I knew it was there. His right arm was in a sling, and the small finger on his left hand was bent at an obscene angle. His right eye glared at me as I sat.

"You know why I am here," I began, "but let's start with the fact that you were all participating in an illegal activity. You should be thanking me that you are alive. I would have been within my rights to kill you all."

"Thank you," he responded sarcastically.

I took a deep breath and smiled at him. "You can be as angry with me as much as you want, but I don't care. I need to know about your cult and if there are any more in Mephosh who follow this heresy.

Wander coughed and spat blood from his mouth. "What more do you need to know? We reject your false gods. We will never worship them."

His stark words took me aback. I was not used to hearing anyone speak of the gods this way. I wanted to chastise him further but now was not the time. His position was clear, and he had paid the price for it. What I needed was to find out if there were any others. "Who else?"

"None. It is just us."

"How can I believe you?" Wander shrugged but then immediately winced in pain. "Where did you first learn of this false religion?"

I could tell that Wander had not anticipated this question as he did not have a quick response. Perhaps the beating rattled his brain as well. Surely this was an answer I would want to know. "Some traders who passed through several months ago. I don't recall their names."

"What were they trading?"

"I don't know. I met them in a pub. I didn't ask."

"These worshipers were in a pub?" I continued. "I know you are lying."

"We don't have the same guidelines that your false religion does. The creator is concerned with how we treat people, not with following an arcane set of rules. We are free to enjoy a pub."

"You would be wise to watch your words," I warned, but Wander only continued to stare at me. "How many others are in Mephosh?" I asked again.

"I told you."

"I suggest that you think harder. If we identify them now, they could potentially escape your fate. However, if they are caught like you, they will also suffer." When Wander failed to answer, I rose. "Very well. We will see if the others corroborate your tale. For your sake, I hope that they do." I left without speaking further.

Next, I went to Kieran's cell. Bruising covered her face, as well as a long cut down her left cheek, and her right ear was mangled. I just shook my head in pity. What a waste of beauty. But at least now Juna would no longer harass me to marry her.

She scowled at me as I asked her questions regarding other heretical groups, but rather than lie to me, she remained silent. Once it became clear that I would get nothing from her, I went to interrogate the others. They had either been well-instructed, or they were truly unaware. If Wander was in fact their leader, it made sense that he had not advised them of other groups. By not knowing, they could not give them away. But I remained convinced that if there was one small group of heretics in Mephosh, there was a good chance of others also existing. And I would find them out.

Chapter 5

THE FOLLOWING DAY I WALKED TO THE PUBLIC SQUARE to find Wander and the other heretics on display, strapped to poles with their hands tied behind their backs. The men's shirts had been stripped away. That served two purposes: showing their wounds from the beating and leaving them exposed to the sun. I quizzed them all again, but they continued to reveal nothing of any other groups. I still did not believe them, but I told myself I would eventually find the others.

Once I was done in the courtyard, I returned to Nikkeudm's chambers. After a brief discussion, I was temporarily relieved from my temple duties and chores. My sole responsibility going forward was to find any other heretics in Mephosh. We would not tolerate false religions here.

For the next few days, I made my way all over the kingdom. I questioned many people as subtly as possible while wearing shabby clothes, as certainly, my efforts would have been in vain if I had been recognized. But, despite that, I learned very little. While rumors might have flown in the marketplace in the past, the news of Wander's discovery made any remaining apostates extra cautious. I heard a few whispers, but further investigation uncovered nothing of value.

As the days wore on and the drought continued, food and water started to be rationed. Some of the well water had to be diverted to the crops so we would not lose them all. My frustration continued to grow as I knew that I had to be correct. There could not have been only that one small faction of Wander's. Yet I was getting nowhere. With each passing day, I became more convinced that the gods' anger would not relent and end the drought until I had eliminated any trace of apostasy in Mephosh.

While I did not need to be in the temple for my priestly duties, I found myself absent from the worship services and skipping my prayers and sacrifices. I also neglected my training, and I had not seen Gallun since my investigation started. In the evenings, I returned home dirty and famished. In my foul mood, my night-time prayers were short and disjointed. I did not know what I was going to do unless I uncovered something soon.

I awoke the following morning with the same poor disposition. I went to the shelf where I had stored my last few jugs of water. The lukewarm liquid tasted stale, and I realized I had been so engrossed in my investigations that I had not visited the last remaining well in some time. The hardened bread I found had turned moldy, and the only other food I could find was a small bag of nuts. I told myself that I would have to go to the market to get my share of what was still available, and perhaps I would attend temple today so I could take some of the leftover sacrifices, if there were any. Plus, it would create a distraction from my growing frustrations.

After relieving myself and dumping the contents with my refuse at the collection site, there was a knock on my door. I opened the portal and found a royal messenger standing before me. Lynna had summoned me to her hall. I told the messenger I would prepare myself and be there shortly, but I was advised that a delay was not recommended and I should leave now. The stern look on his face was unmistakable, so I quickly exited my home.

When I entered the hall, I found Gallun, Nikkeudm, and Oziah, the commander of Mephosh's army, had already arrived. "Good to see you, my friend. It's been a while. I take it by your silence you've not found out anything," Gallun said as we awaited the queen.

"No," I replied, smoothing my cloak and trying to make myself as presentable as possible. "But I am sure there must be more going on here. Wander's group could not have been the only one."

"Do any of you know the meaning of this?" asked Nikkeudm as he slumped his frail body onto one of the benches.

Gallun and I shook our heads as Oziah replied, "I heard that some news was coming out of Su'Meeryn. I don't know what, but obviously, it must be bad." He ran both hands down his long black beard, which was his typical involuntary gesture whenever he was troubled or pondering something. I had known Oziah almost as long as Gallun, but as he had not entered the priesthood, we did not spend much time together these days. His large, muscular frame was covered by red scars like a disjointed map, which was to be expected for someone who spent his entire life as a warrior. He was an affable, friendly man, but he was not to be trifled with. Despite his good nature, his temper was notorious.

The guards began to file into the hall, so we knew Lynna would enter shortly. Nikkeudm's body rose with a creak, and Gallun wrapped his arm around the cleric to help support him. I again smoothed my cloak self-consciously. When Lynna entered, Oziah and I dropped to a knee. Gallun just bowed his head as he continued to support Nikkeudm. After the queen sat on the throne, Oziah and I rose. I could see she was a bit irritated that Gallun had not knelt, but she immediately let it pass. Lynna preferred that all protocols be followed toward her as our monarch. Perhaps not being king put her ill at ease, but she was reasonable and understood the situation.

"Well, I assume you have all heard the news," she began.

"No, majesty," Oziah replied. "I heard there is word from Su'Meeryn, but I do not know what that news is."

Lynna's face scrunched as she shifted her body. "Spies from Su'Meeryn returned last night. The warriors we sent to Su'Meeryn were slaughtered. It seems that Teyon had ordered an ambush. They are all dead."

She stopped and looked at each of us in turn. I could only assume my comrades' shocked faces mirrored my own. Rather than correcting the problem in Su'Meeryn, the plan I had discussed with the queen had actually made the situation worse.

"Why would he do such a thing?" Gallun blurted, but he certainly was not expecting an answer.

I looked at Oziah, but he did not say anything. Why should he? There was nothing to say at this point. The only course of action would be a full-on assault of Su'Meeryn and finally killing Teyon.

"When can the army be mobilized?" the queen asked.

"Two days," Oziah answered without hesitation.

"Good, I expect you three to lead my army. I want Su'Meeryn appropriately punished." Her anger grew with each word she uttered. "And I want Teyon's head delivered to me." I had never seen the queen so passionately resolved as she then turned to Nikkeudm. "As for you, I do not want Sul's investigation stopped while they are gone. You will assign as many priests as necessary to find any other heretics in my realm. Also, I believe we have become too permissive with my subjects and their worship. Perhaps this trial and drought is a punishment from the gods. We need to fully regain their favor. I want you to make sure that all Mephosh completely follows each and every tenet. Am I understood?"

"I will personally see to it, highness," Nikkeudm's thin voice responded steadily.

"Good," the queen stated. Her eyes caught mine, and I thought she would ask me to stay to talk further, but she then dismissed us all. Clearly, nothing else needed to be said. We all knew our tasks. I will admit that I was a bit disappointed that I was not requested to remain. Not that I had any other suggestions, we would need to attack Su'Meeryn with much haste, but I did feel somewhat responsible for the slaughter of our warriors, and I just wanted to offer her support. Since that was not going to occur, I took her last few words to heart. I had let my worship wane during my investigation, and I would need to make penance with the gods before I left for war. I figured two days was enough.

Chapter 6

AS OZIAH HAD PROMISED, we departed Mephosh two days later. We left behind a small contingent of the army with the rest of the priests to remain as protection while the bulk of our forces and all the mercenaries in the queen's employ headed north. The army was too large for every warrior to be on horseback, so the trip would take longer. Servants led carts behind the army with all our supplies and food. I had heard some grumblings that prostitutes had been excluded due to my and Gallun's presence. I knew Gallun was not pleased, but it was fine with me. We needed to do nothing to anger the gods further, and I was still troubled by Lynna's words. I had to refocus and amplify my worship, not slip back into worldly distractions and transgressions.

After breaking for lunch, I went off by myself to offer additional prayers. Gallun was not happy with that either, as he wanted to chat. The gods did not require afternoon prayers, but I felt like I needed to make up for lost time. It was questionable if they would hear me at this time of day as they would be busy with their own activities, but I felt better for it. As I prayed, I looked up at the sky. It was a brilliant blue without a trace of clouds. In a different circumstance, I would have found it beautiful. Now it was just a painful reminder of our predicament.

When I returned to the group, Oziah was waiting for me. I did not see Gallun, so I figured he was off dealing with other matters. "Have you thought anymore regarding our tactics once we reach Su'Meeryn?" Despite being the leader of the army, Oziah knew that he would be deferring to me. As one of the highest-ranking priests, I maintained authority over him, and he was well aware of my intellect.

"I don't think there will be much to concern ourselves with. We did not permit them to rebuild the wall after the last war, and we've only allowed them to maintain a small contingent of warriors. We will slaughter anyone who has a weapon, and then we will make our way to Teyon's hall. He will not survive this time."

I could tell Oziah was not comfortable with my statement, as he felt ill-prepared, but what more was there to discuss? The meager forces remaining in Su'Meeryn were no match for us. We would overwhelm any defense they might attempt to muster. The outcome was not in doubt.

As I grabbed my horse's reins, Gallun approached and asked what we had been discussing. After Oziah had filled him in, he just scoffed. "If they're smart, they won't oppose us at all. They should just throw down all their weapons, and if they don't, we will destroy them."

Oziah was about to reply, but Gallun turned his back and quickly mounted his steed. Oziah looked to me, but I did the same. There was nothing more to say. With Gallun and me leading the way, Oziah ordered the army forward.

We were trekking through the Eusutal Plains. It was a relatively flat land mostly covered with brush. Trees dotted the landscape, and a few now dried-up creeks bisected the area. But the main feature was the tall, flowing grasses. At the right time of day and with the right breeze, it was an exceedingly stunning landscape, despite the relatively benign scenery. When the sun hit the greens, yellows, and browns just right on a breezy day, the reflecting light was dazzling. And if one was lucky enough to find those perfect conditions during the short flowering season in the spring, it was truly breathtaking. However, that was not what we were greeted with on this day as we continued our journey. Spring was well past. The sun was still high, and there was no breeze to cool us off. As we approached one of the still flowing few creeks, Oziah ordered a brief stop to water the horses and give them, and those who were marching, time to cool off.

Gallun was joking with me regarding the entertainment he planned on partaking in once we removed Teyon's head from his shoulders when all around us, soldiers rose from the tall grass, and arrows began to fly.

It took a moment for my brain to process what was happening. Cries began to ring out all around as men fell from their horses. I pulled forth my sword and gave my steed a quick kick, guiding it to the nearest enemy. The man had loosed an arrow and was notching another one, but somehow, he did not notice me approaching. As a second missile flew from his bow, I was on him. He spotted me just in time to see my blade fall. The sharp metal crashed through his bow and sliced his ear. He bellowed in pain as blood poured forth. Weaponless, his hands instinctively rose to the mangled flesh. I swiftly raised my sword, then plunged it into his neck. He stared at me with the knowledge that his life was slipping away. His eyes remained open as he dropped to his knees. I pulled out my weapon as his lifeless body collapsed to the ground.

I turned as, from all directions, arrows continued to fly toward us. After the initial shock of the attack had worn off, our warriors' discipline surfaced. I saw them engaging the enemy where they could. A few small pockets of attackers where engulfed by our troops. The green grass all around was now stained scarlet. A few more of our attackers fell, but almost as soon as it had begun, the battle ended.

On the other side of the creek, we spotted a group speeding away to the north on horseback. As we now were able to examine the aftermath, we saw several holes dug just on this side of the stream and tunnels leading under the shallow river. I sent a few men in, and they emerged from the other side in an area behind a small clump of trees. There, they had dug out a huge pit where they had obviously stored their horses.

This had been an elaborate plan, and clearly, Teyon had begun this construction prior to slaughtering our men. The creek before us was small, but the time required to fabricate and reinforce these tunnels was unknown to me. My anger seethed as I turned my attention back to the army. I learned that we had lost almost a fifth of our men in the attack. We were still a sizable force, but this did hurt us. We had killed a number of their men too, but clearly not proportional.

"I guess this isn't going to be as easy as we thought," Gallun said as he rode up next to me.

Following a brief discussion while I tried to squelch my ire, I agreed that we would delay a short while to burn our dead. I did not want to waste more time, but the gods' directions were clear. We burned our dead to speed up their journey to the afterlife, but we left our enemies for the vultures, rodents, and insects. Their souls could take the long, arduous trek to the afterlife. Besides, I did not want to further tempt the displeasure of the gods. I still felt guilt for how I had neglected them during my investigations back at Mephosh.

Once we got going again, our movements were slower. I would not risk another ambush, but the fact that we were moving through the plains would be to our advantage as there would be very few places for soldiers to hide. We would not fall into the same trap again.

Oziah had ordered scouts ahead as we continued our northward trek. I did not feel like talking, and even Gallun's normally playful demeanor was subdued, so we traveled in relative silence. Scouts occasionally reported back that movements were spotted on the horizon. It was obvious that we were being tracked. That did not bother me, however. Teyon clearly knew we were approaching, and there was nothing he could do that would stop us. It would take us a bit longer to reach

Su'Meeryn, but we would. And Su'Meeryn could not field an army large enough to repulse us, despite our diminished numbers.

When we finally stopped for the night, I was told we had lost a handful of our scouts to spiked pits. I hated losing more men, but at least it was only a few more. Oziah informed me that we would move even slower now since we would need to look for more traps. I was forced to conceal my rage at further delays since my anger would benefit nothing. While we would be traveling slower than originally planned, supplies would not be an issue since we had lost a good number of men. I was not sure a delay would impact the outcome of the forthcoming battle, but I would not underestimate Teyon again. He was trying to delay us for a reason, but for what? He had to know that he could not defeat us. What was I missing?

I awoke the next morning with the same thought churning through my brain, but there was nothing to do about it now. We could not turn around, and I could still not fathom a reason to do so. We would not approach Su'Meeryn fostering the same arrogance as when we had left Mephosh, and I still felt our victory was assured.

The remainder of the trip was uneventful. Oziah decided that he would not send out any more scouts. We would be able to spot any other ambushes or traps, since we knew what we were looking for, and we did manage to locate a few more pits, as the makeshift camouflage was now easy to spot.

Our last night arrived when we were still a few hours away from Su'Meeryn. My mood had improved since we were now so close; any lingering apprehension would be relieved soon. After eating, I sat around a small fire with Gallun and Oziah.

"What do you think is awaiting us when we arrive?" Gallun asked.

"That's hard to say," Oziah replied. "So far, this trip has not progressed remotely as we thought it would."

"True, but certainly, Teyon can't muster a force to stop us, right?"

Oziah took a last swig of his wine before answering, "Not that I can envision."

"Plus, they are fighting against the gods," Gallun continued.

"I suppose so, but you two know more about those things." Oziah dropped his mug and looked over at me. "You are being awfully quiet, Sul. That's not like you."

My gaze turned between my two friends. "I agree with everything you two are saying, but I remain troubled. Teyon can't be stupid enough to think he can stop us, so he must be planning something else. It troubles me that we have no idea what that might be."

"I grant you that," said Oziah. "But I guess we will find out soon enough."

I simply nodded in agreement, then stretched out on my bed roll. It was time for some serious prayer before falling asleep.

***

The next morning arrived all too quickly. The camp was already stirring when I stood. Oziah ordered that the entire army eat a very light breakfast. We would likely be in battle soon, and he did not want any of his soldiers to have heavy stomachs. It was a short time later that we were on our way.

The sun was still low in the sky as we traveled through the plains. It was one of those magical days when the wind blew just enough to set off that dizzying display of colors from the grasses in the rising sunlight. It seemed unmerited that we were given this treat just prior to the killings that were soon to begin.

My heartbeat steadily increased with what seemed each hoof fall from my steed. It felt like it would burst from my chest when we finally saw the outskirts of Su'Meeryn on the horizon. We had arrived.

Chapter 7

SU'MEERYN HAD BEEN A MINOR KINGDOM prior to the last war and being conquered by Mephosh. A small castle for the royal family sat in the middle of the city, which had a wall surrounding it, but our catapults had blasted a hole on the southward-facing side during the assault. Following our victory, Su'Meeryn had not been allowed to rebuild the wall for just such a possibility. Also, all the parapets atop the remainder of the walls had been removed.

As our army approached and the city became more visible, we saw that two large wooden towers had been erected inside the wall. Since we had not brought any siege equipment, we would need to enter the city through the breach. I again cursed myself for our short-sidedness and arrogance. "We should have realized they would have been better prepared," I muttered to nobody in particular. When we got even closer, we all saw logs spread out along our path, and I thought I spotted spikes jutting out from the wood. I briefly wondered where they had obtained those logs from, but that did not matter now. What did matter was the approach would be more difficult than we had assumed, and we would need to be careful.

Oziah ordered a halt and called Gallun and me to his side. "What do you think, gentlemen?" he asked.

"We're going to have to approach on foot, and I'm sure those towers will be filled with archers," answered Gallun.

"And I'm certain we will find other traps along the way," Oziah continued. "I'm wondering if we should return home and come back better equipped. We need our siege engines."

"Absolutely not," I interjected. "Do you want to tell the queen that we came unprepared? She relies on us for our expertise."

"Of course I don't," Oziah barked, "but we are going to lose a lot of good men if we continue forward like this."

"They are soldiers, aren't they?" I continued. "This is what they get paid for. Besides, we will have the gods with us. I will not allow any further delays."

Oziah glared at me. "Keep in mind who leads this army, Sul. My men are not fodder."

"You may lead the army, Oziah, but the army answers to the queen and the temple," I replied coldly. "Your position is not permanent."

Oziah's glare remained. I could not stop him from ordering a retreat, but he knew my threat was real. Despite our long friendship, I would not tolerate being contradicted. That was the power of the priests. Only Lynna held more power than us. One word from me could ruin the life of any person outside the royal family or the priesthood. Perhaps if Oziah had had more personal courage, he would have ordered the retreat, but I knew what his response would be.

"Dismount!" he bellowed. "We attack!"

The horses were brought to the rear with those who handled our supplies, and a few of the soldiers would need to remain back to manage the steeds. Once that had been accomplished, the assault began.

Oziah ordered a small vanguard to lead us out. They were commanded to move slowly and search for any traps. A group of archers warily trailed the vanguard, then Gallun, Oziah, and I led the bulk of our forces.

I watched as the leading men gingerly made their way over the first logs that blocked our path. They had been ordered to signal us if they found anything, but so far, no signal came. When we reached the first log, we did see the spikes that had been driven into the wood. Any slip could be deadly. Since we met no additional obstacles, Oziah sent some men ahead to start moving logs out of our way. After the first few logs were moved, everyone stopped as a signal came up from the vanguard. They gave the sign of a pit and motioned to the right.

Our army began to move to the left. I was apprehensive, as I knew this was planned by the leaders of Su'Meeryn, but we were committed. We would simply need to be careful with our advance. We were still out of range from those hastily constructed towers, and we had avoided most of the other traps that had been made. However, I still had a feeling of trepidation. We lost a few more men to some spiked pits, and soon the arrows would fly. I was certain something else awaited us, but we were almost within striking distance.

Arrows began to rain down from the towers as our soldiers raised shields above their heads, and we continued to push forward. I stayed back to watch the developments, not from cowardice, but because I wanted to see what we were in store for in case I needed to order a change in plans.

The missiles from the walls continued to fall. Many bounced off shields, but some found their targets. The warriors continued on while our own archers hung back to loose volleys toward the towers. I could not tell if any of those arrows found flesh, but if nothing else, they might hamper the enemy.

The first soldiers had reached the opening in the wall, and I began to think that there were no other encumberments, or if there had been, that they had failed. As I began to hear the ring of clashing steel, I started to move forward when I saw movement from the corner of my eye. A few horses had been hidden by what I thought had been debris from the logs. They tore off to the right, then I noticed the same thing to my left. The horses were dragging ropes behind them. It was then I noticed huge nets rising from the tall grass. The nets ensnared scores of our warriors. They cried out, trying to free themselves as a fresh onslaught of arrows and large stones cascaded toward them. Rock crushed bone, and arrows pierced skin as I heard the cries of the wounded and the dying.

I signaled for several nearby men to follow as I sprinted forward. Our trapped soldiers tried to break free from the nets as the barrage continued. Some managed to escape, but many more continued to fall victim to the projectiles cascading down. When we reached the netting, I rushed to the right with a handful of men and sent the others off to the left. With swords drawn, we began to hack at the ropes. The trap had been well constructed, but it did not last much longer. Arrows whistled around us while we cut the ropes. The majority of the missiles continued toward the trapped men, but I heard a thump and a grunt as the man next to me collapsed with an arrow protruding from his right eye. Eventually, all the ropes were severed and the netting dropped, allowing the remaining soldiers to scurry free. Our arrows continued to fly at the towers as the rest of us charged into the city.

Enemy soldiers awaited us as sword struck sword. There were far more defenders than I had anticipated, but we still outnumbered them, despite the heavy losses we suffered to reach this point.

I attacked with an unrestrained frenzy the first defender that I spotted. I leaped forward, and my blade crashed against his. While the man had been ready for that first strike, he clearly was not prepared for a warrior of my skill. My blows hammered down on him until his weapon fell from his hand. He watched it clatter to the ground, then his eyes quickly rose to look into mine. The last thing he saw was my smile as my sword slashed his throat.

One of my soldiers fell next to me, and I quickly turned my attention to his killer. Before that man could celebrate his small victory, my blade severed his left arm at the elbow. His bellow was quickly silenced as I drove my sword through his back. A shower of blood erupted from his mouth as he, too, fell at my feet.

My weapon left a path of death as I made my way through defenders. Unfortunately, many of our soldiers also fell. I spotted Gallun off to my left. His blood-soaked body made a terrifying sight, as the sea of death he left was rivaled only by my own.

I turned my attention back to what was before me a moment too late. An axe had just struck my left thigh. I tried to block out the pain as I confronted my assailant. He was also bloody and had taken a few wounds. His axe rose above his head, but I saw it quiver a bit. What a fool. The weapon was far too large for an extended battle. Between fatigue and his wounds, he could not wield it correctly anymore, and he paid the price. I drove my sword into his belly, and his arms fell behind him while the axe dropped from his grip. As he fell to the ground, I sneered while my blade pierced his heart.

The numbers on both sides continued to dwindle as I spotted Jaleph approaching, attempting to mount a counterattack. I pulled my sword out from the body of my last victim as I moved to meet him. Unfortunately, my left leg buckled, and I dropped to one knee. Thankfully there were no enemies near enough to take advantage of my vulnerability. I managed to rise and quickly examined my leg. Some blood was trickling down, but the wound did not appear too bad. If the man had been smarter and used a proper weapon in the battle, I was certain I would have been far worse off. I took another step forward, and this time my leg held firm. A few more steps caused the pain to intensify, but it was nothing I could not manage.

My sword flicked to the left and right as I approached my prey. Jaleph would not survive this day. He spotted me as I was about to reach him, and with a roar, he sprang. I will admit that I was unprepared for his fury. He sent a dizzying number of blows at me that I barely managed to deflect. His rage was evident, as if I was the person who had caused all this turmoil. To my dismay, he was a far superior swordsman than me, especially with my wounded leg. I was barely able to hold him off, and I lost any sense of the battle that continued around us. His blade seeped through my defenses a few times, but he only managed a few minor cuts. However, I knew that if we were to continue in this melee, he would eventually kill me. I would have to launch a desperate move to try to disarm him, or I would fall soon.

It was at that moment I heard a horn sound from above. Jaleph unleashed a flurry of strikes that knocked me to my knees, but rather than press forward, he turned and ran into the castle. I was dumbfounded. He had me at his mercy, but he fled? As my wits returned, I noticed all the defenders had vanished. I slowly stood as my leg sent rivers of pain up my body. I looked myself over, and every inch of me was covered with blood. There was no way to tell how much was mine and how much was from my victims. I guessed it was irrelevant, except for the fact that I would have to tend to my wounds very quickly.

With the fighting concluded, I tuned back to scrutinize the aftermath. Bodies lay everywhere. Some still convulsed as the last of their lifeblood spilled out. It was a victory, Su'Meeryn was ours, but it would take some time to determine how many men we lost. I could already tell it was a large number.

"I hope you're happy," I heard from behind me.

I spun around as quickly as I could to face a haggard Oziah. He trembled in anger and exhaustion, with streams of scarlet flowing down his long beard. I was in no mood to subject myself to his self-indulgent moralizing at this moment. We had accomplished what we came here to do, what we needed to do. The city was firmly in our hands. If soldiers died accomplishing that task...well, they had done their jobs. As they were fighting to dispatch the heresy against the gods, they would be warmly greeted and rewarded in the afterlife. The gods would be pleased with us and perhaps open up the heavens. Those were my only concerns.

"We are not done yet," I barked. "Search the city for any remnants of defenders. Jaleph and their remaining soldiers may have retreated, but we must find them. And any of the false worshippers. We need to create an example for the rest of the inhabitants."

Chapter 8

WITH THE BATTLE CONCLUDED, Oziah sent out contingents of our men to search the city for any remnants of defenders and to look for signs of where Jaleph and his surviving soldiers had fled. They were also to search for any sign of Teyon, but we were certain he would have disappeared with his cowardly warriors.

A quick count revealed that we had lost approximately sixty percent of our forces since leaving Mephosh. It was a staggering number, and Lynna would be very displeased, but at least we could report that we had been victorious in our mission. It would take time for Mephosh to rebuild our army, but we would certainly plunder the Su'Meeryn treasury. There was no reason to present any pretense of grace to the city going forward.

Now that I had some time, I sat on the ground and examined my wounds. There were scores of cuts on my torso and arms, but nothing serious. My leg was of far more concern. I stripped off my pants and saw the large gash. It was filthy and still bleeding. I quickly bandaged it to stop the flow.

With the fighting concluded, the rest of our group had filtered into the city. I found a medic and braced myself for what would follow. He gestured to me to lay on the ground, then applied some pressure to my wound before removing the soiled bandage. Blood started to flow again as he poured alcohol on the gash, and I could not stifle my cry of pain. He then pulled out a water skin and cleaned it as best he could before pouring more alcohol. With that done, he stitched it up and treated my other cuts. I thanked him as the pain slowly began to subside to a dull ache.

I gingerly stood and began to limp around, looking for Gallun. As I started to worry that he had not survived the combat, I finally found him leaning against a wall. I approached and carefully slid down beside him.

He took a drink of water from a flask, then offered it to me with a weak smile. I gladly accepted and took a long gulp. "You look terrible," he said as I handed the water back to him.

"You're not much better," I quipped.

"A few cuts and a huge bruise on my stomach, but I'll be all right. You?"

"A pretty good slash on my leg and some cuts. I must have lost a lot of blood."

Gallun took another drink before storing the flask away. "Where do you suppose the rest of their troops made off to?"

"I don't know. They must have received assistance from one of the neighboring kingdoms to muster such a force. Pathum is closest, so that would be my first guess."

"Pathum is pretty weak," Gallun pointed out.

"Yeah, and so are we now. We lost a lot of men."

"Was it worth it?"

Aggravation flared, momentarily replacing my pain and exhaustion; surely Gallun was not questioning my decision, too. "We did what we needed to do. We'll strip their treasury of every last coin to hire more mercenaries. And I'm sure that Lynna will conscript some of their young men." I noticed that my tone was a bit sharper than I had intended.

"I'm not questioning that we needed to do this, but I just wonder…" Gallun's voice trailed off as his eyes scanned the bodies strewn about. What more was there to say at this point? With a groan, he raised himself from the ground. His right arm wrapped around his stomach as he tried to mask his pain. He then reached down with his left hand to help me up. I grasped his wrist as he pulled. "Come, my friend," he continued. "If you are strong enough, we still have some work to do." My head spun a bit as I stood, but it quickly passed. I gathered a score of men as we made our way back to the temple.

We marched through the empty streets and spotted a few people peering at us from around corners, but they quickly retreated from our approach. I did not know what we would find when we reached the temple. Would it be empty? Surely these heretics would realize their fate if we found them there, but they were not rational people.

It was only with minor surprise that we found a large group of worshippers kneeling on the ground. Their arms were raised to the sky as their lips moved in silent prayers. The door to the building was open, and I could see that the temple was full. "So Teyon obviously did nothing after we left the last time," I said. "Well, they will pay the price too."

My leg throbbed from the long walk, but I put it out of my mind as I approached the man closest to me. I drew my sword and grabbed him by the collar. "Are you praying to the gods?" I asked. His eyes met mine, but then he turned his head away and back to the sky. He continued his almost silent blubbering, ignoring me. "I will not ask again," I continued. When he failed to respond, I placed my sword point in the center of his neck, then drove it in. As he fell, I removed my dripping blade and grabbed the next man. "And what about you? Are you going to renounce this heresy and return to the gods?" When he, too, ignored me, I kicked him to the ground, then slashed his throat.

Despite these two deaths, there was no change from any of the other heretics. The next one I reached was a woman. She too died under my blade. Gallun moved to another, but I stopped him. My anger seethed through my blood-stained body, and I did not even feel the pain in my leg anymore. If there was any weakness from the blood loss, I did not notice that either. This was a task I wanted to do, I needed to do. I would finish it alone. And if I enjoyed myself, so be it. They brought this on themselves: the ongoing drought and the death of so many of my countrymen.

These fools. They had to be aware of what was happening around them; they could not all be in a trance. But they did nothing to defend themselves. They simply continued as they were, with their eyes and hands to the sky, until they met my blood-drenched sword. After I killed the next few, I did not even bother asking any more questions. I just stepped to my next victim, man or woman—it did not matter. They all deserved the same fate.

It did not take long before they were all dead, and I stood in the temple, like a lone island in a sea of corpses. When it was done, I took a deep breath as the exhaustion returned and almost overwhelmed me. I dropped onto a bench, then ordered my men to empty the building of anything of value. It would all be brought to Mephosh to help rebuild our army. How ironic that we would use any wealth we found here for that purpose. The thought made me smile.

Chapter 9

GALLUN AND I STAYED IN SU'MEERYN FOR ONE DAY. We rested to recover our strength before returning home with about half our surviving forces. Oziah remained with the rest to secure the city. There had been no sign of Teyon, Jaleph, or the rest of their soldiers, so we would not leave the city unguarded. If they did foolishly decide to return, we figured Oziah would have enough men to fight them off.

Oziah would also search for any remnants of this cult of the creator, and he would send some spies out to Pathum for any word of our adversaries. We would confer with the queen upon our return to Mephosh regarding our next steps as Teyon still needed to receive justice. With the plunder we were bringing back, we should be able to at least hire an adequate number of mercenaries, but it would take time to get our army back to full strength.

With such a small number of us returning, we were able to all be on horseback. I was thankful as my body was still quite sore and weak; however, it also meant that I would be subject to much jarring during the trip. Fortunately, the journey was completed without any incident. Gallun and I did not speak much, but that was mostly due to our weakened states. During our brief stops, I pretty much just stretched out on the ground to rest my aching body.

The appearance of the walls of Mephosh was a welcome sight as we rode our weary bodies to the city. I would need a few days of uninterrupted rest to fully recover, but prior to that, I would first have to report to Lynna.

***

The royal hall felt more imposing than usual, and somehow the pristine ceiling seemed even higher when Gallun and I stood before the throne, waiting for Lynna to emerge from her chambers. When she did,

I saw a look of concern cross her face at the sight of us. "Where is Oziah?" asked the queen. "Did he survive?"

"Yes, majesty," Gallun responded. "He is alive. He has remained in Su'Meeryn to manage the city until you assign someone to that position."

"I see. Well, tell me, what happened."

Gallun was about to continue until I placed my hand on his arm. I would be the one who would advise the queen of our victory and our failures. When I had finished my tale, I could see her doing all she could to control her anger. She ordered one of her servants to bring her a goblet of wine before she spoke again.

"It seems you men thought too highly of yourselves. I am extremely displeased to hear of all these losses. We will have to send messengers out immediately to hire more mercenaries. I don't want any of our neighbors to think that we are an easy target now."

"My queen, I know you are displeased, and you have every reason to be, but it will take time for news of this to spread. Teyon most certainly fled north, and he will be too worried about his own survival right now. Besides, none of our neighbors are particularly strong or have much inclination towards hostilities towards us," I stated.

"I suppose you are correct, but I am still not happy that I have been put into this position."

"At least we took the city," Gallun interjected.

Lynna turned a sharp eye to my friend. Her glare was unmistakable, and I could tell that Gallun immediately regretted his words. With a wave of her hand, she dismissed him. "Return to the temple and see what tasks Nikkeudm has for you." With a moan, Gallun bowed, then quickly exited the hall. I did not know if I should feel sorry or envy him as I remained before our incensed queen. "I'm unsure whether or not I should ask for further advice from you, Sul, but what are your thoughts regarding our next step?"

"If I may, majesty, I am not a fool. I know we suffered heavy losses, and we should have been better prepared. But, even if we had, I honestly do not know if we could have pursued a different course. We needed to fully conquer Su'Meeryn after the actions of Teyon."

She glared at me, obviously not sure how to respond. The silence became more and more uncomfortable as she finished her wine. "I am not a fool either, Sul," she hissed. "I may not have the experience to know tactics, but it seems to me we should not have lost so many men against such a smaller force."

I knew that I had to take a gamble and push my point a bit further to keep myself in her good graces. However, the wrong words might bring about the opposite effect. I could lose her trust if I contradicted her too much, but she was a reasonable woman, especially if I could make my point. "You are correct, but perhaps only marginally. They had the advantage that they were in the city and protecting it from us. They also had time to prepare. Nothing we could have done would have changed any of that."

"Yes, but you still should have been better prepared. You could have taken the extra time and brought the catapults and towers." She stopped for a moment to regain her composure. "What do you propose that we do next? I want Teyon dead."

"You are correct, majesty. Teyon must have secured assistance from somewhere. Pathum is the closest kingdom, and the army that met us was too large to have been solely from Su'Meeryn. I suggest that we hire mercenaries as quickly as possible and that Gallun and I lead them back north. Oziah should stay where he is as your new regent while we hunt them down. I doubt that they are far away. I assume that they will be scheming for an opportunity to retake Su'Meeryn."

Lynna nodded in agreement. "As soon as you are ready, I want you back on the road. I'm trusting you with this task, Sul." She rose and started on her way back to the chambers but then turned around with a stern look on her face. "Oh, and I do not want to see you in Mephosh again until you complete the task I previously gave you. I want Teyon's head. Am I understood?"

"Of course, my queen."

With that, she turned again and left me standing alone in the hall. I knew her statement was a thinly veiled threat, but it made no difference to me. I would miss the temple and my worship duties while I was gone, but I was now singularly focused. Even though I had the sense Jaleph might be the real menace, I had no desire to return home until I had located and killed Teyon.

***

I spent the next two days alone in my small home. It was good to finally strip off my filthy clothes and wash off all the remaining traces of blood on my still-sore body, which needed the rest. A few stitches had popped on my thigh, but the wound was healing. I saw no sign of infection. Now that I was back and resting, I would be able to spend some concerted time in prayer.

Despite our sacrifices and victory over the heretics, the gods still had not granted us rain, and the situation was becoming dire. More of our crops were beginning to wither. If we did not have rain soon, the land would experience a full-on famine. That thought only increased my anger at Teyon, Jaleph, and all of Su'Meeryn. I was becoming increasingly convinced that the gods were punishing the entire land due to the abomination of this cult.

After those few days of rest, I finally felt strong enough to emerge from my home. I was thankful to make my way to the temple pain-free. After all the combat, I was anxious to resume my priestly duties and offer sacrifices to the gods. I did not know when we would muster enough men to head out again to war, so I wanted to enjoy this time to focus strictly on my religious tasks. Upon my arrival at the temple, I found Gallun there, already tending to the doves.

"Good to see you, my friend," Gallun said once he spotted me. "I was beginning to worry."

"I thank you for your concern. I just needed some time to rest and seek favor from the gods. This drought is becoming very concerning."

"Indeed. Did you hear about Wander and the others?" I shook my head as I lit a candle and grabbed a dove from one of the cages. "While we were gone, they all escaped. Apparently, some of the heretics helped free them while attentions were divided."

I placed the struggling bird on a small altar and carefully slit its throat while pushing this new aggravation away for the moment. The blood trickled down, and I purposely kept my hands away. I had little desire for more blood to reach my hands. The time would come soon when that would occur again, but there was no need to rush it. Once all the blood had drained, I knelt on the ground with the bird above my head. I prayed the gods would direct me in my mission to rid these lands of the false worshippers, and I prayed they would find us worthy to once again allow the rains to fall.

With my prayer completed, I stood and placed the dead bird amongst the others from the previous rituals. "It's just a matter of time before we find Wander, Teyon, and the others. And when we do, they will not bother us again."

"You are correct there," Gallun replied with a grin. "Now, come. We have many waiting for us to perform the worship service."

As we headed out of the sacrifice room and started towards the sanctuary, Nikkeudm shambled up to us, his joints popping with each labored step. "Ah, there you are. I'm glad to see that you are feeling better, Sul. Don't get too comfortable, as you both will be leaving much sooner than you had anticipated."

"What do you mean?" asked Gallun.

"It turns out that most of the leaders of the mercenaries were in Mephosh when you were gone. They assumed their services might be required imminently, and they are a very opportunistic group. The bulk of their soldiers are already on their way here. So, most likely, you will be heading back out in only a few days."

While I had been looking forward to spending some more time strictly with my worship, the news pleased me. I was anxious to draw my sword again and strike down the remaining apostates. Once we had eradicated them all, I felt certain the gods would finally relent and open the heavens again for the much-needed nourishing waters to feed our lands.

***

I spent most of the next few days either at the temple or at Gallun's home. The rituals of the gods were enjoyable, and we all continued to beseech them for rain, but I knew it was fruitless. Their anger remained, and there was only one way to squelch it: the death of Teyon and the others. Even the evenings at Gallun's home were becoming tiresome. I enjoyed being with my friend and his family, but we discussed the same issues every day.

The meals had become much smaller as Lynna had ordered stricter rationing of all food and drink. Even our gambling lost its appeal due to the tasks that lay before us. I was not sure I would find any enjoyment in my life until Teyon's head had left his body, preferably by my sword.

It was with much delight when Gallun and I were informed that the bulk of the mercenaries had arrived. We would depart soon with them and about half of our remaining soldiers. While the mercenary code was staunch, and they never betrayed those who paid them, Lynna still felt better that we had some of our own men with us. And I cannot say that I blamed her. I could not fully trust those I did not know, especially a group that was notoriously secular.

The evening before we were to leave, Gallun and I met with Ithar, the man who had been selected to be the leader of the mercenaries. There were several different groups whom the queen had employed, but I had asked that one individual be elected to speak for them all.

Ithar was a tall, slender man with shoulder-length dark hair and a dark complexion. A long scar ran from his temple to his chin, which disrupted the right side of his thin black beard. He wore a black jacket and black pants. Even his scabbard was completely black. The only bright color he exhibited was his piercing blue eyes. One moment those eyes seemed to portray an aura of malevolence, while the next moment, they seemed warm and inviting. He exuded an air of pride that put me off. I immediately disliked him.

"So, you are Sul," he stated as he sat in one of the chairs in the priests' study, far too comfortably for my tastes. "I'm told we will be taking our orders from you."

"Yes, I am in charge. You will be under my command as well as Gallun here. He is my closest friend and also a priest. You will defer to him as well."

"Of course, whatever you say." Ithar's smile seemed far too jovial, and my displeasure grew.

"Do you have a problem with that?" Gallun asked. He was obviously aggravated as well. "You and your men are being paid handsomely."

"I mean no disrespect," answered Ithar. "It's just that my men and I have been in countless campaigns. They are rightfully, how should I say…concerned about being led into battle by priests."

My anger dissipated somewhat. Ithar and his men had no idea who Gallun and I were. They had every right to be apprehensive of us as their leaders. "You and your men may rest assured that while we are priests, we are also warriors. We have been in many wars ourselves. Gallun and I are actually the finest swordsmen in all of Mephosh."

"Yes," Gallun continued for me. "We were in the last battle at Su'Meeryn, and many of their soldiers fell under our blades."

The blue eyes softened ever so slightly as Ithar contemplated our words. "Very good. I will reassure the men that we are in good hands. Our code binds us to your queen, but it will be good for our morale knowing that we are not following a couple of fools. It is reassuring that we will not likely have to take matters into our own hands once hostilities start."

"What does that mean?" Gallun asked sharply.

"Lynna is our employer, not you two. If you are found to be incompetent, I will not hesitate to kill you both and continue the mission as the leader." Ithar's tone did not change as he made his explanation, and his eyes continued to exhibit the appearance of warmth.

"I appreciate knowing your position," I replied, mimicking his matter-of-fact tone. "But you may rest assured that that will not be necessary."

"Very good, then," he continued as he rose from his chair. "Then there is nothing further to discuss. I will see you gentlemen in the morning."

***

The following dawn found me riding north from Mephosh once again. Our force was smaller this time as we were not expecting to attack a city. Even if Teyon and his men were hiding in Pathum, we had no plans to start a war with them. Since our entire contingent was on horseback, we would not have the trailing supply group, so we all had to carry our own provisions. Normally that would not be an issue, but with the ongoing drought, resupplying along the way might be a problem.

Fortunately, it was a short trip back to Su'Meeryn, and we could top off supplies there. After that, we would be on our own, and we did not know what we would find upon arrival in Pathum.

The grasses of the Eusutal Plains were far more brittle than they had been when Gallun and I last traveled through. Shades of brown and beige were the only colors I saw in every direction. I even ordered a stop so the two of us could offer up prayers. We had not yet put an end to the apostasy, but we pled to the gods to find favor with us in our mission. But as expected, no rain came. I remained convinced the drought would persist until all the heretics were killed. Ithar watched us pray with a bemused grin. Any delay meant little to him. The mercenaries were paid by the day, so we could linger as long as we wanted. He just shrugged when Gallun and I remounted and continued north.

Upon reaching Su'Meeryn, the mercenaries quickly dispersed to visit the pubs and brothels. They were not known for being frugal with their earnings. Gallun was eager to join them, but I told him I would not be partaking in any revelry during the mission. I had been questioning my piety, and I wanted the gods to find nothing lacking in me while I continued to beseech them for rain. I also told him that, as a priest, I would not allow him to partake either. He was very displeased with that statement, and I had no assurance that he would follow my command. But command him was all I could do. I was not responsible for the choices he made.

With Ithar and the others on their way to their debauchery, Gallun and I sought out Oziah. We found him in what had been the royal dining room, where he was just finishing up his dinner.

He looked surprised when he spotted us walking in. "What are you two doing here?" he asked.

I briefly advised him about the mercenary army and that we wanted to replenish our supplies before heading out in the morning. I then questioned him about what had transpired in Su'Meeryn since we had left.

He handed his empty plate to a server and wiped his mouth on his sleeve. "Well, we found a few more of these heretics and put them to death. Following the battle and the slaughter, most of the people were willing to help us. Many of them blamed the cultists for the drought and were pleased to see more of them die. So, holding the city should not be an issue. I don't foresee the citizens giving us any problems."

"What about your spies?" I asked. "Any word regarding Teyon?"

Oziah's fingers combed down his beard, away from his frown. "No, nothing. I find that odd and troubling. We should have at least heard something."

"Yes, I agree. That is strange," I replied.

After a pause, Gallun asked, "Might you be able to spare a small number of your soldiers for our mission?"

"That should be fine. We are starting to conscript some of the young men. Many aren't happy about that, but we are managing."

"Very good," I responded. "Please prepare us some rooms for the night and have whomever you assign to us ready to leave in the morning. If you could provide us with supper, that would be much appreciated."

"Of course," Oziah said as he waved to a server to bring more food. "It won't be the amount that you are used to. We are rationing what little we have."

"We understand. Lynna has been doing the same thing back home," Gallun said. "But provide us what you can in supplies before we leave."

"I will. Now, if you will excuse me, I need to meet with some of the nobles. There has been much squabbling about their new roles since the battle. I will see you both in the morning."

"Thank you," I replied as Oziah headed out of the hall. When Gallun and I had finished eating, we said our good nights, and I went off to my room to complete my evening prayers. Gallun said he would do the same, but I did not believe him. I was certain he would find his way to the nearest tavern and the welcoming arms of a high-priced wench.

Once I entered, I was grateful for the solitude of a quiet room. I had one of the servants bring me a dove so I could offer a sacrifice along with my nighttime prayers. The sacrifice was not necessary, but I continued to do all I could to sway the favor of the gods. With my religious duties completed, I stretched out on the soft bed and promptly fell asleep.

***

Light began to trickle in through the one window in the room, signaling the arrival of morning. I rose from bed with the anticipation of the new day. We would be back on our horses shortly, on our way to Pathum. I fully expected that we would find conflict in that small kingdom, and I was looking forward to putting an end to these heretics once and for all. If the king of Pathum was not a fool, he wouldn't oppose me.

Chapter 10

THE TREK FROM SU'MEERYN TO PATHUM was a bit shorter than Mephosh to Su'Meeryn. We were in the northernmost outskirts of the Eusutal Plains. To the east, low foothills started to develop, and more trees began to pop up, heralding the forests north of Pathum. While I was well-schooled in the geography of this area, I had never before traveled north of Su'Meeryn.

With each passing day, the land showed greater effects from the drought. The grasses we rode through were even more withered than what we had encountered in the south. The trees we saw seemed to stand wearily, giving the appearance of wrestlers after a hard-fought match. If the gods did not relinquish their anger soon, I did not know what any of the kingdoms would do. We would have to start transporting water from the river to the west, and that would be a huge ordeal to bring enough to make a difference.

As we rode, Gallun abandoned any pretense regarding his activities of the previous night. While he regaled me with stories of his depravity, I was scarcely listening. I was angered that he had not devoted himself to a pious night, but I could not remain angry that he acted in a way that was true to his nature.

As I was about to tell Gallun to stop talking, Ithar rode up alongside us. "Ah, my friend Gallun, it is good to see you again. We had quite a night last night, did we not? The morning definitely came far too early. Had I known how entertaining priests could be, I might have found religion in my youth." He laughed heartily at his own joke as he reached over and slapped Gallun on his back. "But I did notice your absence, Sul."

"Some of us needed to be pleading with the gods to give us rain," I quipped.

Ithar just laughed again. "So you think the gods care about your pleas? You are indeed a funny man. What a wonderful mission this is. I'm learning more and more about priests each day."

"Do not mock me," I responded coldly.

"You misunderstand me, my friend. I'm not mocking you. I appreciate that I knew so little about priests before meeting you two."

I still did not approve of his tone, and I was prepared to bark at him further when Gallun interjected. "Sul and I had not spent much time with mercenaries before now either. We've always had some in our armies, but not to this current extent. It's always good to learn from each other, isn't it?"

For a third time, Ithar laughed heartily before riding off, and I found it disconcerting that Gallun was the one who had stepped in to placate a tense situation. While I was a man never known for having a long temper, Gallun had always been the more volatile of us two. This incident only reinforced the growing concern that my piety was diminishing just when Mephosh and the whole land needed it most.

***

When we reached Pathum, it was decided that Gallun and I would ride in to seek an audience with the king. We wanted to give him an opportunity to respond to our inquiries prior to starting any hostilities. We had to be careful, as Mephosh could ill afford war, but I was certain Pathum would not want to risk the ire of both Mephosh and Su'Meeryn.

With our army waiting outside the city walls, we were ushered through the gate. The guards eyed us suspiciously as we dismounted, and we handed a pair of them our reins. "Follow me," a third man said as he began to lead us down the main street.

Pathum was a kingdom smaller than Mephosh, perhaps about the size of Su'Meeryn, I assumed, although I did not know for certain. I was aware that Pathum was the primary trading port for the northern kingdoms of Okkgan and Unimeth due to the easy trip through the plains south to Su'Meeryn and Mephosh. Since Mephosh was the largest kingdom in the land, Pathum would not want to anger Lynna by doing something foolish to Gallun and me. Without our trade, their king would lose much of his wealth.

When we reached the royal hall, we were greeted by their king, Zalah, and his queen, Athan. As customary, the thrones were at the back of the hall, but the royal couple did not occupy them. I found this strange as it would be expected for the monarchs to be on their thrones to greet emissaries from a foreign kingdom. Instead, the pair walked along the side of the room, examining the candles embedded in sconces on the wall. "These are getting too low," Athan commented. "We will need to have new ones brought in."

"Excuse me, highnesses," the guard said, "but I bring you Sul and Gallun, priests from Mephosh. They have requested an audience."

The king waved the man away as a number of royal guards emerged from the shadows with swords drawn. I immediately felt some apprehension, but the guards did not approach us any further and just stared at us.

"So, you are the two leading an army to my kingdom?" Zalah said, more of a statement than a question.

"No threat intended, majesty," I replied as calmly as I could manage. "Mephosh intends no ill-will towards our friends in Pathum. As we are sure you have heard, our vassal Teyon in Su'Meeryn has rebelled against his queen, Lynna. He has attacked her troops and must be brought to justice."

"Yes, we have heard the sad news, but what does this have to do with us?" asked Athan.

I was a bit put aback that the queen had interjected herself into the conversation, but Zalah did not seem concerned. He just strolled over to his throne and took a seat while the queen remained by the candles.

"We believe that Teyon and his conspirators may have sought refuge in Pathum," Gallun answered.

"That is quite an assumption," continued the queen. "What makes you think that?"

"It is only logical," I replied. "Pathum is the nearest kingdom to Su'Meeryn. After we defeated their forces, they fled to the north."

"Well, you are correct there," Athan stated as a servant handed her a new candle, and she placed it in an empty slot. "They did come to our lands. We found them a beaten and bloody mess. My husband advised them that we would never risk the ire of Queen Lynna, and we sent them on their way."

"Why didn't you imprison them?" asked Gallun.

Athan let out a snort. "While they may not be our friends, they are also not our enemies. We respect Lynna very much, but we are not allied with her. We did not offer them any help before they departed. It was not our place to hold them."

"Yes, and my spies have determined that they continued north towards Amyon," the king added. "From what they were able to determine, Teyon and his men are still there."

"We thank you for the information," I said. "Lynna will be very pleased to hear of your support in this matter. She is very generous to all those who aid her. Now, may I ask for a bit more assistance? It would also be very much appreciated if you might replenish some of our supplies."

"Our apologies, but we will have to decline that request," Athan answered as she removed a small candle from its holder. She extinguished the flame and placed the candle in the pocket of her yellow gown. "We are aware that the drought is as bad to the south as it is here, but we must save all the provisions we have for our own army and subjects."

I eyed the pair with skepticism. I did not doubt the drought was impacting Pathum as much as Mephosh, but I found it questionable that they could spare nothing for us. Glancing at the king, I noted what I took as an expression of ignorance. Turning back to Athan, I felt a sense of ire directed at Gallun and me.

"The forest thickens north of us," she continued. "You may be able to find game there, and perhaps the streams have not yet all dried up. Apart from that, is there anything else we can offer the troops of our friend Lynna?"

"I don't believe so. We thank you for the information that you have provided, and we will be certain to let our queen know of your hospitality." I hoped they caught the sarcasm in my words, but I could not tell if they did. With nothing else to say, Gallun and I excused ourselves and exited the chambers. We were escorted to the gate, retrieved our horses, and rode back out to our army. After advising Ithar of the information we received, we immediately continued our trek north. This time, Amyon was our destination.

Chapter 11

AS WE LEFT THE VICINITY OF PATHUM, the land became more rugged, and the trees grew taller and denser. I knew we would be riding through forest, but I was not prepared for the rough ground. Ithar only laughed at me when I complained about it. "You priests don't get out much, huh?" he quipped.

"We have more important things to do than travel," Gallun retorted playfully, to my displeasure. It was clear they had become friendlier after their night of debauchery. "Someone needs to petition the gods."

Ithar glanced about at the withering trees. "Doesn't seem to be helping much," he continued with a grin.

Gallun's mood soured immediately at Ithar's comment. He spat to the side angrily before continuing. "Now listen, you can—"

"Enough!" I commanded, interrupting my friend. "We all have our jobs to do, and we will do them once we find Teyon."

"That will have to happen in the near future. Otherwise, we are turning back," the mercenary leader stated.

"What do you mean? You are being paid handsomely, and you'll finish your task," Gallun responded.

Ithar's faux jovial manner immediately dissolved. "We mercenaries take our responsibilities very seriously. But unless we finish our job promptly, or you are able to resupply this army, we return to Mephosh. As you are aware, we will be running low on food and water soon. We will return some of the gold to Lynna, but our oath does not include starving ourselves."

"You knew what you were signing up for," I pointed out. "The drought and our supply issues were well known."

"That is true, but you did say you expected to find your quarry in Pathum. That did not happen, and you have no plans that I can see to resolve the food and water problem if we need to continue much further."

Gallun's face had begun to glow a deep shade of red when I interjected, "Your point is taken. We will see what happens when we reach Amyon. Perhaps they have supplies they can offer or sell. Maybe the drought is less severe there, or perhaps we will find Teyon. We will reassess our situation at that time. We do not need to come to any hasty conclusions."

Both Gallun and Ithar appeared mildly appeased with my statement. Ithar just huffed what sounded like an affirmation as he slowed his horse so he could drop back with his men. "I don't like him," Gallun muttered when he was gone.

"You seemed to like him well enough before his comment about the gods," I said, "but he's not wrong. If we are not able to conclude our mission soon, we will have to decide how to resupply and proceed, as Lynna has made it clear that we are not to return unsuccessful."

"So what do you propose if we don't find Teyon in Amyon?"

"Well, right now, I'm not proposing anything. If we have to continue on from Amyon, we'll need to spend some time in prayer first and seek direction from the gods. But we will not be able to return home. Lynna certainly would not welcome us back."

Gallun clearly wanted to respond, but he had nothing to add. His mind was not currently sharp, which I attributed to his lack of sufficient sleep. His quick temper with Ithar and his inability to properly assess our predicament concerned me, but there was nothing I could do about it now. And we both knew our circumstances. We knew we could not return to Mephosh if Teyon still lived, but our supply situation would eventually become dire. At this moment, I was at a loss.

***

For the next few hours, our journey proceeded in silence. I continued to ponder our quandary, as did Gallun. Our looming difficulties, along with this unrelenting drought, only amplified my anger with these heretics. While I was not averse to undertaking arduous tasks for the gods, I could not help but wonder what I would be doing at this moment if not for Teyon and the others. I would likely be in the temple, administering a sacrifice or praying with a congregant, with a full mug of refreshing water beside me.

As my mind drifted, I was not paying too much attention to my surroundings. The northern trail continued through the trees, and I did not notice the hills to each side. We reached a dried-up creek bed that bisected the hills when suddenly scores of arrows rained down on us from each side. I heard cries of pain and the thud of men falling from their steeds.

"Ambush!" Gallun bellowed as we all whipped the shields from our backs to defend ourselves from this deadly onslaught.

Our own archers pulled out their bows and sent arrows in every direction, but they had no clear targets at which to aim. The aerial melee continued for a time until a signal rang forth, and soldiers charged at us from the trees, surrounding us on both sides. I unsheathed my sword and spurred my horse to the left. My blade met my first adversary, crushing down on his helmet. I heard a grunt as he collapsed, and I immediately diverted my attention from him to my next foe. His sword reached up to mine with the crash of steel.

Our attackers were all on foot, which was somewhat of an advantage in the rough terrain. I did not have much room to maneuver my horse, and the rocky ground was difficult on the beast, but it quickly became a non-issue as a pike speared the animal in the chest. The horse squealed in pain and bucked. Blood poured from the wound, and I knew I needed to dismount before it collapsed, pinning me under its bulk. I jumped off, losing my shield in the process, and rolled away. I was back on my feet before any of the enemy managed to take advantage of my predicament.

With sword in hand, I sprung at my next victim. He was ready for my move and deflected my blow. I struck again only to find his own sword blocking mine. Again and again I tried, but I could not breach his defense. As I continued to push at him, I became vaguely aware of the sound of the combat all around me. I heard the ringing of sword against sword and the cries of the dying. I had no idea which side was winning the battle, but I was unable to investigate. I had to focus solely on my opponent.

I momentarily stopped my assault as I began to circle him. He eyed me, clearly pleased with himself. I could sense his smugness, and instinctively, I knew that would be his undoing. I struck again, but this time in a clumsy manner. He easily defended himself. I attacked a couple more times, each time allowing him to fend me off. I saw the confidence on his face grow; he figured he had me. He now pressed his own attack. I blocked him but gave the impression that my defense was far more difficult than it actually was. He continued to push with a prideful appearance, believing I would fall soon, but his last attempt was sloppy in his overconfidence. My arm shot out like lightning as I knocked his blade from his hand. His expression of confidence quickly dissolved to dismay as he realized his error. But his realization did not last long as my sword pierced his chest.

With my adversary dead, I spun about to take stock of the combat. I spotted Gallun, along with a few of the mercenaries fending off the attackers from the east. The rays of the lowering sun were reflecting off the blood-stained blades as they rose and fell. It appeared that just about all our men were on foot now. All along the trail, every man was engaged in the battle. It was too chaotic to tell which side had the upper hand.

The fact that we had been ambushed in this way was dumbfounding, but I did not have the time to consider how it had occurred. I heard the sounds of approach and had to quickly swing around to face my next opponent.

Two men rushed at me. Their swords were held high in eager anticipation; however, they were amateurs. I quickly side-stepped both, and my sword slashed the torso of one. He bellowed in agony as his entrails spilled from his gut. The other man turned towards me, but his foot slipped in the gore of his companion. He spun about for a moment before falling to one knee. His sword dropped from his hand as he gazed up at me in dismay. I merely smiled as I plunged my blade into his face.

With those two now dispatched, I looked up, and with much shock and delight, I saw Teyon standing before me. He was gasping for air, covered in blood, his sword ready to strike.

A chuckle of glee escaped my lips as I leaped for my prey. Any thought of failing my queen evaporated from my mind as my sword danced toward his throat. Teyon blocked my blow and tried for a counterattack. My blade easily deflected his, and I could tell he was no match for me. The smile on my face grew as I knew Teyon would soon be dead. I had no idea how the battle would turn out, but the regent would certainly not survive.

In the distance, I thought I heard a call to assist the king, but the sounds of the battle encircling me drowned out the words. I felt the desire to toy with my quarry, much like a dog with a caught rodent before its jaws crushed the life from its victim, but I could not risk extending this melee. A foe could catch me from behind, or my foot might slip in the muck and blood. Following a few more parried blows, I moved in for the kill. With a speed Teyon had not expected, three sharp blows dislodged his weapon. His sword rattled to the ground,

Weaponless, Teyon lunged at me. I twisted away, and my left hand pushed him off balance. He stumbled, and my left foot kicked out. I caught him on the knee, and he fell face-first into the crimson mud. Before he could rise, I pounced and drove my sword point into the base of his neck. His body went limp as his blood poured forth onto the ground to mix with all the rest. I wanted to complete my mission and hack his head from his body, but that would have to wait. The combat continued, and we would have to bring it to an end before I could undertake that final task.

As I stood from Teyon's lifeless form, I found an enraged Jaleph looming before me. His muscular body heaved in huge breaths at the sight of the dead regent, the man who at one time had been Jaleph's king.

Jaleph sprang, and based on our last encounter, I was, for the first time in this battle, concerned. Very few men in the whole region could best me with a sword, and I knew that Jaleph was one of them. His blade erupted at me, and I barely managed to deflect it. My only hope was that his anger would hamper his skill. He continued to push forward, and with much difficulty, I was able to keep his weapon away from my flesh. A slight stumble allowed me to shoot past his defense, but I only nicked his upper arm.

Following a very brief instant to regain himself, Jaleph unleashed the most ferocious attack that I had ever witnessed. With the speed of a wolf, he pummeled me with blow after blow. All I could do was try to keep his sword at bay, but it was useless. My arm grew numb from his mighty strikes. Eventually, my arm collapsed, and both our weapons crashed against my skull. I roared in agony as pain exploded in my head. A bright white flash filled my vision, but it almost immediately dropped away as blackness fell upon me like a curtain at the end of a play. My knees buckled as I dropped to the ground. As the pain increased, all I could see was blackness.

My mind was vaguely aware that I no longer held my weapon. I was confused. My fingers frantically searched about for it. Not that it would do me any good if I did manage to locate it, as I still saw nothing. I tried to look up while my hands patted the wet ground, when a new wave of pain burst from my right shoulder. I felt what must have been Jaleph's sword enter my flesh. The weapon burrowed in further as the agony overwhelmed me. My stomach heaved, and vomit spewed from my mouth as I finally, mercifully, lost consciousness.

Chapter 12

I SLOWLY STARTED TO AWAKEN, and that was extremely unpleasant. My body ached all over, and I felt a searing pain in my right shoulder. I opened my eyes, but no light came, no color, only blackness. I brought my hands to my face and rubbed my eyes, but that accomplished nothing. I dropped my arms to my sides, which only caused the agony in my shoulder to increase. It was then that I realized that I was lying in a bed.

My mind drifted back to the battle. How had I come here? Where was I? I reached to my shoulder and felt a bandage. Clearly, someone had attended to my wound and brought me to this place to recover. I could only imagine that we had been victorious and that I had been taken back to Pathum, hopefully by Gallun.

I tried to sit up, but the pain shot down my arm so much that I cried out. It was then I noticed how dry my mouth was. I fell back into the bed, and my panic increased. My vision was gone, and all I felt was misery. I took some solace in the knowledge that we had been successful, and I most assuredly had won the favor of the gods. Whether I was to live the rest of my life in agony, I would at least have this victory.

When I fell back into bed, the pain subsided somewhat, and I noticed I was extremely hungry. I wanted to stand, but I had no idea where I was or anything about my surroundings. And since I could not see, that did not seem like a good idea. I figured since someone had brought me here, there must be people nearby. "Hey!" I cried out. "Hey! Is anybody there?"

My call brought no response, so I shouted again. Still nothing. After calling a third time, I perceived some muffled sounds of movement. Then I heard a door open, and what sounded like two people entered the room.

"Ah, I see you are awake," a deep voice stated. It sounded familiar, but I could not place it. "We were not sure for a while if you would survive. You lost a lot of blood."

"Who are you?" I asked.

"You don't recognize me?"

"I've lost my sight. I can't see anything."

"Hmm," the man replied. "That is interesting."

"I still don't know why he's here," a woman interjected. "We should have let him die."

My panic grew even more. Who were these people, and where was Gallun? Teyon was dead, but how had the combat ended? I questioned my assumption that I had been taken back to Pathum following a victorious battle. I had no sense of where I was or who I was with. These people had obviously saved my life, but were they the enemy? If they were my enemies, why had they saved me? Blindness was torturous enough, but the thought of being in the hands of the heretics made it even worse.

"The conflict was over," the man continued. "His death would have served no purpose."

"True, but what purpose does his life serve?" she asked.

There was a pause that I found extremely uncomfortable before the response came. "That will eventually become evident."

Trying to push the thoughts of my predicament aside for a moment, I decided to interject myself into their discussion. "While you are deciding my fate, might I trouble you for some water and some food?"

"You do know that we are in the midst of a drought, don't you?" the woman responded.

"Of course."

"Come now," the man said. "We have put droplets of water into your mouth these past few days, but obviously, you need some nourishment. I will have a small amount brought to you. You don't want to rush this." The voice was familiar, but I still could not identify who it was.

"Thank you. Your kindness is much appreciated." The woman snorted, and I heard what I assumed was the sound of her stomping away. "I seem to know your voice," I continued, "but I cannot place it. Who are you?"

"There will be time for that soon, but for now, I will take my leave. Someone will return shortly with food and drink."

I was left alone again, and hopelessness crashed down on me. I was blind, in constant pain, and in the grip of my enemies. I could only assume my future would become worse.

***

After an unknown amount of time, a miniscule meal was brought to me. A short while after that, I heard someone enter my room again. I instinctively looked up, but I still saw nothing. "Who's there?" I called out.

"So you don't recognize our voices, do you, Sul?" It was the woman who had come to my room earlier.

"I don't recognize your voice, but the man did sound familiar."

"That was Wander, and I'm Kieran."

The names impacted me much like Jaleph's sword before I had lost consciousness. The heretics I had ordered the beatings of back in Mephosh had escaped to here, wherever here was. And apparently, they were the ones who had saved my life. I was dumbfounded. "How? Why?" was all I could stammer.

"That is a good question," she answered. "It was Wander's decision, not mine."

I tried to regain my composure, as I knew I was not giving a good, priestly appearance. With an excruciating effort, I resituated myself in the bed. "Let's move back. What happened in the battle after I fell?"

"From what I was told, after you killed Teyon," her voice almost hissed as she spoke. "After you fell, both sides spiraled into disarray. Gallun and the others managed to secure Teyon's body, then immediately withdrew. It was assumed you were dead. Wander was the one who discovered that you lived."

"Where are we, and what are you two doing here?"

"We are in Amyon. This is where we escaped to after being freed from the stocks in Mephosh."

"But how?"

"You pagan priests and your pride. You think those of us who worship the creator are a fringe group. But you are very much mistaken. We might be a small contingent in Mephosh, but we have great numbers in Pathum and Amyon. Their kings renounced your false gods years ago. You think the king of Pathum aided you? Ha. It was all part of Wander's plan. They led you into the ambush."

I had a hard time processing her words. Nobody had spoken to me so bluntly before. If this had happened in Mephosh, Kieran would have been thrown into the dungeon. I never would let anyone address me or the gods in this manner, but I was in no position to chastise her. I also had no reason to disbelieve her. But it was still very confusing. Why would these two I had beaten and left imprisoned in Mephosh save my life? Well, clearly, it was not Kieran's decision.

"What is to become of me? Did you save me just to torture and then execute me?"

"We do not act in that manner. Wander has made it known that you are not to be mistreated in any way. Once you have recovered enough, I have no idea what his plan is." I felt her hand take hold of my right arm, causing my shoulder to burn in agony, and I cried out. She quickly released me and apologized. "I forgot about your wound."

After a moment, she grasped my left arm and helped me stand. "Wander says you need to start moving, and your soiled bedding needs to be cleaned. I will take you to relieve yourself, and we will walk as much as you can." I appreciated her kindness, but I heard no tenderness in her words. I certainly did not expect any after how I had treated her and her companions.

Once I was up, it felt good to be moving, but I was very stiff, and my body ached. My shoulder throbbed, but the pain was manageable if I did not move it too much. I wanted to thank her, but I could not bring myself to do so. She was still an apostate, and it was because of these heretics I was in the position I found myself. And then there was my vision. My blindness terrified me. I tried to push the thought away, hoping it would only be temporary, but I had no idea whether that would turn out to be true.

The stroll through what I assumed was the castle of Amyon went longer than I had thought it would. We did not say much to each other. Even though I could not see her, I clearly sensed the tension between us. Once we returned to my room, Kieran said that others would come to check on me until they felt I was strong enough.

"For what?" I asked.

"I don't know. That was all Wander said."

"You defer much to Wander. Why is that? Who is he to you?"

"Wander is a great man, far more than an armorer. It is unfortunate you and your kind never saw that." I had no response to her proclamation.

After I was back in bed, I realized the room smelled much better. I guessed I had been in my filth for so long that I had not noticed the stench. Still baffled by my situation, I spent time in prayer. I begged that the gods would restore my sight and heal my shoulder. I wanted to petition for my escape from Amyon, but I thought that might be too presumptuous. The gods can be fickle, after all. I was not in immediate danger, and my blindness was my primary concern. After I concluded my prayers, I eventually managed to drift off to sleep.

***

The next few days found a steady stream of others coming to my room. They were all pleasant to me, helping me care for myself and move about. With each passing day, I felt a bit stronger and all the aches in my body began to subside except for my shoulder. That pain always remained despite numerous pleadings to the gods. That and my blindness.

All this still made no sense to me. Every time I asked why I was here, I always received the same cryptic response: Wander had ordered it. Who was he to these people? He obviously held some high position in this cult, but how had that come to be?

The fresh water and minuscule portions of food I received every day were another mystery. There was a window opposite my bed, and I could hear the sounds of the outside, so I knew that still, no rain had fallen. Why would these people continue to deliver these essentials to an enemy when certainly they had better uses for them? I was grateful for the sustenance but could not fathom why they had saved me.

It was on one of the following mornings that I awoke, and I do not know if it was a sense or I unknowingly heard soft breathing but I knew someone was in my room. "Who's there?" I asked.

"I hear you are well enough to travel now. You will come with me."

"Wander," I said. "Where are we going?"

"Outside."

I felt his hand grasp my left wrist, and I stood from the bed. After preparing myself and eating a few pieces of bread, he led me out of the castle. It felt nice to finally escape those cold walls, but the sense that I was in an open space and still could not see was extremely disconcerting. While the pain in my shoulder was somewhat manageable, it had not decreased in the last day or two. The thought of never being able to see again troubled me greatly, along with the fact that the gods had brought no healing or rain. I had killed Teyon. What more did they expect from me? What more did I need to do to earn their favor?

"Where are we going?" I asked again.

"Come," was his only response.

We walked for a short while, and the noises of the kingdom lessened with each step. When those sounds had faded to a slight murmur, Wander stopped me. I felt him coaxing me to sit. When we were both on the ground, and my back was against a tree, Wander began:

"I know you have questioned why I saved you and why you were brought here. You cannot fathom why those you had beaten and almost killed would offer you this kindness. Well, it is quite simple, but the problem is your deceived mind cannot comprehend it. I do not blame you for your past deeds. You have only done what you thought you must, with your misguided morality.

"You know nothing except the lie of the gods. This falsehood was perpetrated on you; how could you have acted differently? I don't fault people for being ignorant."

While I remained helpless in the clutches of these apostates, his words angered me to the point that I briefly forgot the despair of my blindness and pain. I could not let that statement stand, even though I was entirely at the large man's mercy. "I am far from ignorant," I retorted harshly.

"You are an intelligent man, Sul, in your way. But not knowing truth is, in fact, ignorance. I am here to show you the truth."

A laugh burst from my lips. Even if I had wanted to stop it, I would have been unable to. "You, a heretic, are going to teach me? I am a high priest of the gods."

"What is funny, Sul, is that you think of the word heretic as an insult." Wander's voice remained calm and soothing. "I take no offense with a pagan calling me such. In actuality, I view it as a compliment. But let us not get bogged down in that debate for the moment. Let me ask you a question. What have the gods done for you?"

"What?" I asked, somewhat dumbfounded. It was such a silly query. "The gods owe me nothing. I am their servant. What has your creator done for you?"

"That is a good question, and I will answer it. But first, what have the gods done for you? Anything?"

I paused for a moment to gather my thoughts. "I am their priest. They have given me my life and my position. All that I have, all that I am, I owe to them."

"No, they haven't given you anything," Wander continued. "Nikkeudm was the one who gave you your position, and your mother gave you life. None of this comes from the gods."

"I assume you will tell me that all this started with your creator?"

"Right now, I am saying nothing about the creator. What about the drought? Have the gods brought rain? What about your vision? Are you still blind? How many prayers have you offered up regarding those? What exactly have your gods done for you?"

"And what has your creator done? You can spew your false doctrine all you want, but I can turn it back on you. Has your creator brought rain? What about Kieran's and your beatings? Did your god stop those?" My rage grew at the man I felt was responsible for all my suffering, as well as the suffering of the land. "I watched all those worshippers in Su'Meeryn pray as my sword took their lives. Why did your creator not stop me?" I was practically shouting when I finished my diatribe. I took a few breaths to attempt to calm myself. If I had my vision, I would have glared at the man, and that reminder only increased my anger. But I had to remember I was still at his mercy.

After a pause, Wander calmly continued. "I think we can agree that the gods have not ended the drought and restored your vision. Can you at least concede to that?" I nodded, which I assumed he could see. "What if I told you both of those held a purpose, and you are the key to that purpose?"

"What are you babbling about?"

"I will admit that the drought concerned me greatly for a time. The creator's will was difficult to see during that period. The beating I received was what brought me clarity. When I was placed on display in Mephosh, it was then that He spoke to me. He told me that you were the key, and this was the moment you would understand.

I laughed again at the ravings of this moron. "You are a fool, and you have obviously always been a fool. All of you are fools. I desire no part of whatever this is that you saved me for."

This time, Wander laughed at me. But it was not a sarcastic laugh such as I had directed toward him. "You are about to experience the creator's power," the large man stated, then he became silent.

I sat quietly. My rage still seethed. I wanted to spit at Wander due to the position I found myself in. If not for these heretics, I never would have suffered the blow that took my sight, and I would not have this constant pain in my arm. Despite his words, I was coming to believe he had saved my life only to toy with me. I resolved myself that I would say nothing until Wander spoke next, then I would laugh in his face. If he decided to kill me after that, so be it. I did not want to subject myself to the lunacy of this madman anymore. I would no longer play this ridiculous game with him or any of these other fools.

As the fury in me continued to grow, from overhead, I heard a rumbling. The noise distracted me from my pity as the warm air began to cool against my skin. The rumbling grew louder as I felt my heartbeat quicken. Along with the roaring, the wind began to howl. An energy surrounded me as I felt the hairs on my arm stand on end. My anger morphed to fear, as I could not imagine what was happening to me now. I finally recognized the sound of thunder as the crashes rattled in my ears.

Rain began to fall in waves. It soaked my body as the gale-force wind whipped it around. I was instantly soaked, and my body began to shiver. The water struck me so hard that the pain in my shoulder grew. I tried to stand, but my body refused to move, as if the rain had pinned me to the ground. I could not comprehend what was happening all around me.

Then I sensed Wander stand, and I heard him cry out, "Now, experience the power of the creator!" An even louder crash of thunder ripped through my head and rattled my bones. What I could only assume were the branches of the tree I sat under fell and struck my body along with the rivers of rain. My hands went to my ears as a flash of light engulfed my eyes. My head felt like it was ablaze, and I screamed in agony. I sprung from the ground just as the pain in my head immediately disappeared. The white light dissolved to reveal Wander's face beaming at me through the streaming rain.

"And now you know," he stated. His arm wrapped around me as he led me away. I glanced back and saw the smoldering embers in the tree quickly being extinguished by the continuing rain. We walked back to the castle without speaking. I had no idea what to say. I watched as the inhabitants of Amyon danced about and splashed in the welcomed water.

My whole life had just changed, but in that moment, I had no idea what any of it meant.

Chapter 13

WANDER BROUGHT ME BACK TO MY ROOM, and he told me he would leave me to spend some time alone with my bewilderment, pondering what had just happened. After he closed the door, I stripped out of my drenched clothes and dropped onto my bed. The fresh scent of a recently cleaned room reached my nose, and I glanced about, finally able to examine my dwelling.

The room itself was nondescript, but what caught my interest were the couple of murals that hung on the walls. They displayed congregants worshipping what I could only assume was their creator. I had never seen religious artwork before that did not depict the gods. I found this striking. In the past, this would have been extremely annoying to me. But after what I had just experienced, I was merely confused.

I turned away from the murals and sprawled on the bed. As the sound of the rain continued to seep through my window, I rubbed my eyes. While I was grateful to have my vision restored, how had this happened? Was Wander responsible for it?

My arm still ached, and I wondered why, if my blindness had been healed, why not my shoulder too? If Wander or his creator could restore my sight and cause the rain to finally fall, why not completely heal me? I could find no logic in that fact.

I rubbed at my shoulder as my mind swirled. My thoughts turned to Gallun. I had known him longer than I could remember. We had grown up together, gone through religious and military training together. He had been my closest friend my entire life, a life that had been devoted to the service of the gods. That service spanned the mundane of cleaning the temple to the killing of our enemies. What did this mean regarding our friendship? He was like a brother to me. I had been fully devoted to the gods and to my city. I loved Mephosh and was completely dedicated to Lynna. But how could that continue after what I had just experienced?

With a groan, I stood from the bed and walked over to the window. Peering through the opening, I watched the rain continue to fall, and I saw a few people still celebrating along the street. I reached out and let the water pelt my hand. It was cool and refreshing. The long drought was over. I thought of all the prayers I had offered, all the pleadings and sacrifices. Had they been fruitless? My mind could not cope with the thought that my entire life had been dedicated to a lie. The weight of that notion crushed down on me like an avalanche, and I began to weep.

As the tears streamed down my cheeks, I returned to the bed. Evening was approaching, and I just wanted to sleep. Perhaps the following day would bring me some clarity, a new perspective. I collapsed on the soft mattress, still crying. Normally I would spend time in prayer prior to sleep, but no prayers entered my troubled brain. Who could I pray to, and what would I even be able to pray for?

Despite my exhaustion, sleep eluded me for a very long time. The tears that streamed down my face mirrored the rainwater that continued to fall on the other side of my wall. My spiraling consciousness finally drifted off sometime before dawn.

***

A rattle at my door aroused me from my slumber. Being awakened frustrated me, as I would again have to face the dilemma of what I had experienced. I rose, grabbed a robe from the wall, and found Kieran on the other side of the portal. She had a tray of breads and fruits in her hands along with a goblet of water. "Here is your breakfast," she stated, and I still detected a tone of animosity in her voice. "Prepare yourself, and I will be back shortly. Wander has instructed me regarding matters we need to discuss."

"Where is Wander?" I asked, wondering if this battered woman noticed my dejected tone.

"He is busy with other matters." She thrust the tray harshly at me and retreated down the hallway.

I placed the plate on the small table beside my bed, relieved myself, then gratefully devoured the food, as I had not eaten much the previous day. When the tray was cleared, I placed it outside my door, then dressed. Once done, I sat on the one small chair in the room and awaited Kieran's return, brooding on what this new day had in store for me. I was certainly glad to no longer be blind, and I was thankful for the rain. However, being powerless was disconcerting after the might and structure of my life to this point.

It was not much longer before Kieran was back at my door. I offered to let her in, but she said it would not be appropriate for her to stay alone in my room with me. She wordlessly led me down the castle corridors. The few people we passed eyed me suspiciously, but nobody said anything. Kieran took me into the large dining hall. As breakfast had already concluded, only a few people remained. She led me to an empty table and motioned for me to sit.

"I'm sure you realize how uncomfortable this is for me," she began. "While I'm very pleased that the drought is over, it is not pleasant to be conversing with the man responsible for my beating." She paused, apparently awaiting a reply, but what was I to say? Yes, I had ordered the beating of Wander and her; nothing would change that fact. When I remained silent, she continued. "Wander says that I should not blame you, that you were only doing what you had to as a priest. I understand that, but that does not make this any easier."

Kieran hesitated again. I still did not feel that there was anything I could say, but I did not want to make her any more uncomfortable than she already was. "I understand," was all I could muster.

"Wander says that he has forgiven you and that I must as well. I know he's right, but it remains a struggle for me."

Her words were strange to my ears. Why should they forgive me? The gods demanded loyalty, obedience, and respect. There was nothing in their tradition that called for forgiving an enemy. In fact, we always preached the opposite. Enemies of the gods were to be dealt with swiftly and without mercy. Absolution was a meaningless concept to them.

"Now tell me, what do you think of the events you have just experienced?" she continued.

My mind started to drift back to my devotion to the gods and that the woman before me was an apostate and an enemy, but the fact that I could see her reminded me of the previous day. After those events, how could I continue to hold on to my pride and piety? "Honestly, I don't know what to make of my situation. Did Wander cause all this?"

Kieran laughed at my words. "You still don't understand?"

"Enlighten me."

She took a deep breath and folded her hands on the table. "Wander didn't cause the rain to fall or your sight to be restored. He is a prophet of the creator. Perhaps the greatest in all the lands. Wander was told that, for some reason, you are important to our plans. The drought was trying for us all, but Wander knew something would come of it. And also that there was a purpose for your blindness. You were healed at the same moment the drought ended. Certainly, you can't attribute that to coincidence."

"I'm well aware of that."

"Well, then, what are you going to do with those facts? You must admit that your gods had nothing to do with it."

"I know," I replied softly, and this time I was certain she heard the hopelessness in my voice. All I felt was despair as I pondered my past. I still desired to hold onto my faith in the gods. But I sensed that faith dissolving. It was slipping through my fingers, much like the rainwater when I held my hand out the window the previous day.

"After the death of my husband," Kieran continued, "Wander approached me in the market and asked me to work with him in the armory. I initially refused. Why should a noblewoman humble herself in that way? I still had a little wealth, and I was being courted by many, even before the funeral. He later requested an audience. I suppose he sensed a willingness in me to question the religion of the gods. He took quite a risk in confiding his faith to someone he did not know very well.

"As he persisted, something in his demeanor and words persuaded me. I had no desire to work in the armory, but it seemed the best place to receive instruction from him. He showed me how the gods are nothing more than a fable. I know how difficult it is to realize you have been living your entire life for a falsehood. You do realize it's a lie now?"

The question struck me like the club that had smashed her ear. I looked into her pretty eyes and knew that I could even see her at all proved her point. The gods had done nothing to end the drought. The gods did not heal me. There was no way I could deny what I had experienced under that tree. "Yes." That was all I could force out my mouth, and the word crushed me. I felt my entire life being pulled from my grip.

For the first time, I noticed a semblance of a smile on her face. "Very good," she said. "Now, what will you do with that truth?"

"What do you mean?"

"If you have come to terms with the fact that the gods are a lie, what will you do now?"

That query was another crushing blow. It was difficult enough to admit that everything I had devoted myself to was a lie, but my whole life centered on that belief. With that belief now shattered, what was I to do? How does a man of my age and stature start over? "I have no idea."

"Good, that is what I wanted to hear."

"Why is that good?"

"Because you will be open to the possibilities."

"I see." But in truth, I did not.

Kieran then leaned back in her chair. Her face, which had slowly started to brighten, suddenly turned dour. "There is one more factor that you have to consider."

"What is that?"

"If your life has been governed by a myth, then so were your prior actions. How do you cope with those?"

I looked at her face. Her left ear was still contorted from the thrashing she had received, and her right cheek was now deformed. She tried to camouflage it with cosmetics, but she failed. She was still attractive, but not to the degree that she had been. I then thought of Wander and his beating. How had my life brought me to that point? And what about Su'Meeryn? So many soldiers lost their lives because of the battles to squash the heretics. The memory of all the death and the blood I had wrought swept over me like a tidal wave.

Then I thought of the temple in Su'Meeryn: those worshippers of the creator. I had killed them all. I had not let anyone else participate in that slaughter. Looking down at my hands, I realized that every one of those deaths had been caused by them. No one else's. The hands I now saw so clearly. It was all me. I was a slayer of the innocent, a butcher of the oppressed. I was the wickedest man that had ever existed. I had killed for a lie, and I had taken joy in it. Why had I been saved? Why had I not died on that battlefield? Why had their creator spared and healed me?

The emotions built up until I could no longer contain them. They exploded from me like an erupting volcano. My head fell into my hands as sobs of sorrow and regret poured from my eyes and mouth. I wanted to speak, tried to speak, but to no avail. What was there for me to say anyway? I continued to weep uncontrollably. Perhaps Kieran placed her hand on my wrist, but I was not certain. Nothing around me registered to my senses. Guilt and sorrow were the only perceptions I experienced. Visions of my victims cascaded over me in waves.

My sobbing continued. I do not know how long I sat there. Time lost all meaning. As my body heaved, streaks of agony flowed from my shoulder. The pain seemed appropriate. With all the misery I had caused, why shouldn't I experience the same?

At some point, I was finally able to gather a bit of control. I wiped my face with my sleeve as I managed to utter a couple words. "I'm sorry."

"I forgive you," Kieran stated after a long pause. Her absolution should have softened my despair, but it only caused me to weep harder.

After I marshaled some additional composure, Kieran led me from the dining chamber. If some onlookers remained, I had no idea. I was certain at least a few other people had been witnesses to my display, but

I did not care. If I had made a spectacle of myself, it only seemed appropriate, if not reciprocal to my deeds.

We made our way through the castle, but I had no notion of where we might be going. And I did not bother to ask. The future seemed meaningless. What could be waiting for me, and what difference did it make? My past could not be erased; the images of my victims remained. I did not care what the future held. How could someone who had committed such atrocities care about his future?

Kieran eventually stopped at a door and motioned toward it. The stab of pain from my shoulder almost did not register in my brain as I opened the portal. I walked into a small room full of books and scrolls. There was a table in the middle, and opposite me sat Wander. He looked up as I entered. There was a chair on the other side of the table, which he motioned for me to take. As I sat, Kieran followed me in, closed the door, and sat in another chair in the corner of the room.

It was strange to see scrolls opened before Wander. I only knew him as the armorer in Mephosh, and most people in his position would not have learned to read. Only the priests and nobility received schooling. All others would have spent their youth training in their vocation and nothing else. "We must have had a breakthrough if Kieran has brought you to me," the huge man stated.

"It was much as you had expected," Kieran responded.

"Good. That is very good. Now we can begin." Wander then turned his attention to me. "I take it you have seen the error of your prior ways?"

"Yes," I said softly. I felt the emotions boiling up inside me again, but I resolved myself that I would maintain my composure. I would not create a similar scene to what had recently occurred.

Wander obviously saw the turmoil on my face. He paused to give me a moment as I took a few deep breaths. "I am certain it's been difficult to see your entire worldview upended like this. But you are now starting to take the appropriate steps."

"What do you mean by that?" I asked as my sorrow started to morph into exasperation. I was tired of his riddles. It was all becoming too much for me to endure. "Why did you save me? You should have let me die on that battlefield. What good can come of this? If you thought restoring my life was a kindness, you are mistaken."

A soft chuckle escaped Wander's lips. "No, my friend, it was not out of kindness that we saved you. And I do not envy you the life that you will live now. Your past deeds will always be a part of you, and I pity you for that. However, you are vital to the creator's plans going forward."

Vital? Me? How could that be so? My thoughts swirled as my irritation turned back to despair. I was a wretched man. I should be taken out with the refuse, discarded for the dogs to devour. I absently shook my head at Wander's soft gaze. "And what might that be?" was all I could say, but I really did not want an answer to my question.

"I have an idea, but It's not fully clear yet. All I know is that you will serve a purpose." With that, Wander rose from the table and commanded me to follow him. In my previous life, I would have chafed at being ordered around by a man in his position, but not on this day. The arrogant priest who commanded respect out of fear no longer existed. I knew that I needed to redefine myself. However, I wondered how that was even possible. While Kieran and Wander may have forgiven me, I remained haunted.

We exited the small study. Wander led, and Kieran followed after me. Those who passed by obviously knew who I was, and they all seemed to glance at me with malice and suspicion. A few days ago, this would have bothered me as well, but now I almost relished their disdain. I had earned it, after all.

Following a short walk, we entered a corridor that grew in size as we continued. The hallway came to an end at a huge double door. Two men, obviously royal guards, stood on each side. Large torches blazed next to each guard. A quick glance revealed small windows in the ceiling and on the walls for the smoke to escape. There must have been some means to block out the rain that had recently fallen, but I saw no evidence of that.

"We are expected," Wander stated. One of the guards nodded, and both doors were opened before us.

A great chamber was revealed to me as we stepped in. We trod on a narrow orange rug that bisected the room. It was wide enough for perhaps two people. Candles all along the walls and large windows filled the chamber with light, but what struck me was the utter lack of any decoration or adornments. There were no signs of wealth or prestige anywhere. How could this be the hall of a monarch? After we traversed the sparse room, we stood before the throne. Although the seat itself was carved with intricate designs, in the places where jewels once sat, I saw only holes.

Sitting upon the chair was the most ancient man I had ever met. A few threads of wispy hair escaped his otherwise bald, wrinkled head and trailed below his shoulders. His thin face gave me the impression of a cadaver, and his blue robe hung loosely from his stick-like arms. Yet his gray eyes sparkled in the bright light, and I could tell that, despite his age and appearance, this was not a man to be trifled with.

To his left was a very small, empty chair, and to his right was the queen's throne. The woman who sat there was less than half the king's age. She wore a dark, unspectacular gown and no jewelry. But her appearance was striking nonetheless. Thick, yellow hair cascaded from her smooth white face. Even without cosmetics, her beauty was evident. She smiled at Wander, but the expression soured when her gaze turned to me.

"Highnesses, may I present Sul, the former priest of Mephosh," my dark-skinned companion began. "Sul, please bow to his majesty, King Typheus, and his bride, Queen Phillemy."

Wander placed his hand on my shoulder, and I immediately regretted standing to his left as the pain ignited in my shoulder. I tried to ignore it as I took a knee before the couple.

"Rise," the withered voice of Typheus commanded. As I stood, he continued, "You are fortunate that I have much respect for you, Wander. I still am displeased having a man such as this in my kingdom."

"If you are unhappy, imagine how I feel," a familiar voice said, and I saw Jaleph emerge from the shadows of the back of the chamber. It made me wonder if this day could possibly become any worse.

"I appreciate your indulgence with me, but I'm confident that the end of the drought has brought me some latitude. And you did not free me from Mephosh without purpose," Wander stated.

"You were right about the drought." Typheus' thin voice cracked. "But what do you propose at this time? Why bring this vile pagan before us?"

"It is well known that Sul is one of the most fearsome warriors in all the land, perhaps second only to our good friend Jaleph here. With the army of Mephosh weakened, we should call upon all your allies to assist Jaleph in finally freeing Su'Meeryn from the pagan clutches of Lynna. Once that is done, Mephosh will be the last kingdom under the grip of the false gods.

"Sul should ride beside Jaleph for the attack. The former great priest of the gods now riding with us to vanquish those very gods. This will be a tremendous symbol to any who still question the true faith."

"You must be joking," Jaleph spat. "After all this man has done, he should be dead. I acquiesced to you due to your reputation, Wander. Saving him was one thing, which I did not agree with, but riding alongside me? Absolutely not!"

"We must put aside our grudges and our pride for the good of the creator," Wander continued. "Do not forget what this man has done to both Kieran and me. We have forgiven him, and—"

"I don't care what you've done or didn't do," interrupted Jaleph. "Sul killed my king and I don't know how many other Su'Meeryn citizens. It is only by a tremendous effort that I allow him to stand before me."

"Be careful how you speak in our hall, Jaleph," the queen interjected. "We may all be allies in the faith, but you stand before the throne of Amyon."

Jaleph took a breath to calm himself. "I mean no disrespect to the king or the queen, but I must be honest: you do not rule me. I will abide by your commands while in your castle, but you have no authority over me when I leave here. Sul will not ride with me." He furiously crossed his arms over his chest to emphasize his point.

"Please, Jaleph," Wander continued. "We must—"

Jaleph interrupted again. "I must do nothing! You may be a revered prophet, Wander, but you have no authority over me either."

"If I may," I heard Kieran say from behind me as she stepped forward. "Look at my face, at my ear. Sul ordered the beatings of Wander, me, and the others, and he enjoyed it. I know that doesn't compare to all the people he killed in Su'Meeryn, but I too have been wronged. I wanted him dead just as much as you, Jaleph.

"However, I was with him when he came to terms with his past. Once he understood that all he had lived for was a lie, he was devastated. He understands the weight of his deeds, and the memories of the dead will haunt him for the rest of his days. As he said to Wander, he knows that us saving him wasn't a mercy. Yet if we claim to live by the faith we profess, we are compelled to forgive him."

Jaleph huffed at her comment, and his turmoil was evident. He turned to me with disdain, "What say you, priest?"

I did not want to say anything. Kieran and Wander had forgiven me, but I had not requested it of them. "After all I have done, Jaleph, asking for your forgiveness is something I could never do. These two have forgiven me, but that was solely their choice. All I can say is that while I remain alive, I will do whatever I can to make amends for my past. However, there is an issue no one has addressed. While my vision was restored, my shoulder did not experience healing as well. Every time I move my arm, pain rips through me. I don't see how I could possibly fight."

Jaleph laughed at my statement, and I could see that his face had softened, if only a fraction. He stood still for a few heartbeats as all eyes turned to him. "So be it," he said. "I will take him with me. Yes, Sul, you will fight. And if it causes you pain, all the better. Your pain will be a constant reminder of all your sins."

Chapter 14

I STOOD IN THE COURTYARD OF THE CASTLE of Amyon with Jaleph before me. His sword was drawn as his eyes burrowed into mine. With an agonizing breath, I awkwardly drew my own blade. I did not understand how anybody thought I could enter combat if I could barely brandish my weapon.

A clang of steel amplified my pain as my sword fell from my hand. Jaleph's glare remained. I could tell he wanted to strike again, but he restrained himself. Rather than retrieve my sword, I turned and walked to a bench on the side of the yard. I dropped onto the seat with feelings of defeat adding to my guilt.

Jaleph gave me a look of disgust before exiting the courtyard without a word. Kieran, who had accompanied us, retrieved my blade, then sat beside me. I gratefully took the weapon and placed it on my lap. "Anything I can do to help all of you," I started, "but I don't know what that could be if I can't even hold a sword."

"Give it a bit of time," she answered. "Your injury wasn't too long ago. I'm sure you will be able to do your part. Wander is never wrong about these things."

"If I'm supposed to fight, why wasn't my shoulder healed along with my vision?" It still made no sense to me.

Kieran sighed. "I don't know. Even Wander doesn't know. Perhaps it is as Jaleph said. Maybe it is to be a reminder of your past."

"If so, that seems pretty cruel."

"Your past was cruel."

I could not disagree with her, but that led me to another troubling issue. "Everyone continues to talk about my past, and rightfully so. Yet now it seems everyone wants me to repeat my past. You all want me to kill again."

"It is different this time," Kieran replied after a pause. "You are not being asked to kill innocent people. Mephosh has invaded and conquered Su'Meeryn. Jaleph is only looking to free his land from pagan rule. That is the best way to stop further innocents from being killed."

"Will he then turn his sights on Mephosh?" I flipped the sword over and examined its edge. It unquestionably needed sharpening. "Lynna still rules there, and they will continue to worship the gods."

"Most of the other kingdoms have denied the pagan religion. Once Su'Meeryn is free, Mephosh will likely not be far behind."

This troubled me. While I had been purged of any belief in the gods, I still maintained my loyalty to my homeland and my queen. "I could never raise a weapon against Mephosh or Lynna. I love them both."

Kieran gently placed her hand on my arm, and the tenderness of the gesture startled me. My head turned to study her expression. Certainly, this woman, who had suffered much due to my past, was not developing feelings for me. I instantly knew that this was not the case. Her expression was one of sorrow and pity, not attraction. "No one is asking you to. I can't speak for Jaleph or Wander, but I don't believe they would ever sanction an attack on Mephosh."

"That is good to hear, but I still don't see how I will ever be able to fight again."

***

Over the next few days, I returned to the courtyard to spar with Jaleph. Kieran always accompanied me, though I did not understand why she would spend so much time with us. The combat continued to go poorly. Everyone knew my skills with the sword, but I was currently worse than a novice. I even tried to switch hands a few times, but that did not go any better. How could I possibly be of any value to anyone?

Somehow, Jaleph showed enormous patience with me, but he also displayed some delight. He was obviously enjoying my pain and frustration. Yet as I struggled, I thought I was starting to gain some of his respect for persevering through my misery. During our many breaks, we even started to chat. I discussed being raised in the priesthood while he talked about his youth in Su'Meeryn and how he had heard of the creator from Pathum merchants. He was surprised when he had learned that stories of the creator predated the belief in the gods, but as the pagan religion had spread, any knowledge of the creator had been eliminated. I found that interesting, as I had always been a student of history, yet nothing in the documents in the temple at Mephosh told a similar tale. I guessed that was not surprising since we priests had been tasked with suppressing anything which might challenge the gods.

Kieran would sit with us during those breaks, and she would school me in their theology when it seemed appropriate, and Jaleph seemed to be learning almost as much as me. While he had rejected paganism years ago, he had never spent much time learning the new doctrine.

What struck me most was when Kieran discussed the creator's love for all of creation. The gods were not worshipped due to mutual love. They were worshipped out of fear and respect. She then talked of how one's devotion brought about forgiveness for our many transgressions.

This remained a difficult concept for me to accept. Each twinge of pain down my arm brought forth memories of my victims. While Wander and Kieran may have offered me their forgiveness, how could I receive absolution from the divine? I had completely rejected any notion of the gods, but my current mindset had been formed by that pagan belief. The capricious nature of the gods left little room for compassion or reconciliation.

"Surely my sinful past is much too great to be exonerated," I dejectedly said to her during one of our discussions.

"There is no scale with the creator," she replied, and I noticed a stunned look on Jaleph's face. Forgiveness was evidently an attribute he still struggled with as well.

"I… I…" My stammering confirmed my confusion as I looked at her scar and mangled ear. Turning to Jaleph, I thought of Teyon falling under my sword. Then I thought of all those worshippers I had slain in Su'Meeryn. How could there be no scale? How could the enormity of my sins be exonerated? My shoulder stung as I stood. "If you say so," I replied in a condescending tone that I instantly regretted. My intent was not to patronize her. I only needed to get my mind off this troubling subject; it was too painful for me to dwell on. All that mattered now was my commitment to Jaleph and the liberation of Su'Meeryn. "Let's return to it," I said to Jaleph as I readied myself.

As the days went by, Kieran continued to attend the sparring sessions, and I was beginning to understand her motivations. While she had made herself responsible for me, it was Jaleph who truly occupied her interest. And I could tell that he returned the attraction. This knowledge gave me some solace. I was pleased to see these two individuals I had so immensely wronged find some peace, some pleasure together.

With each passing session, my pain diminished a bit more. It did not disappear, but it was manageable enough that I was not hindered in combat. Every time my blade met Jaleph's, the ache increased, but perhaps I was becoming used to it, so I was able to force my way through.

Following our sparring, I would return to the small room which had been provided to me. The exhaustion would overcome me, allowing sleep to arrive promptly. That was a blessing, as it relieved my pain and silenced my guilt.

After about another week, the pain seemed to have plateaued. It had not disappeared, but I was able to fight at the level I had before the injury. I was still no match for Jaleph, but I was confident I could be of service in the attempt to retake Su'Meeryn. The zeal I once displayed for the gods had morphed into a zeal to rid the land of this pagan religion, but I did not relish the thought of going back into combat or subjecting myself to the agony of my shoulder. However, I was resolved to it. If the only consequence of my past was this pain, I would gladly accept it.

***

Now that my retraining was complete, our focus turned to preparing for the assault on Su'Meeryn. The kingdoms of Pathum, Okkgan, and Unimeth had all previously rejected the pagan gods and had pledged support to this effort. Emissaries had been sent to those lands to strategize the attack. The plan was to assemble the largest force possible, but only large enough that all could travel on horseback. If the assembled army would have to move on foot, Su'Meeryn would most certainly have time to prepare a strong defense. Jaleph was confident that any spies currently in Amyon had nothing to report. If the fact that I was alive had been made known in Su'Meeryn or Mephosh, it would not have provided them with any information.

Once the assault was ready, the armies would ride out as quickly as possible and meet in Pathum, then join up to rush towards Su'Meeryn. The goal was to reach Su'Meeryn before any spies could sound the alarm. Also, a small contingent had already been sent out and ordered to camp just north of Su'Meeryn. Their task was to intercept any potential spies heading for the castle.

As Jaleph worked with the military commanders of Amyon to prepare their forces, I was summoned to meet with King Typheus and Phillemy. When I reached the hall, it was empty except for the royal couple and a few guards. I was again surprised by the sparseness of the immense room. As I walked in, Kieran also entered and trotted up beside me.

The king and queen were not seated on their thrones this time. They were at a small table on the far side of the hall, playing a game with dice and cards that I was unfamiliar with. When they saw Kieran and me, they motioned us over to sit with them.

"You were not summoned, Kieran, but I'm pleased to see you," Typheus began in his thin, cracked voice.

Feeling a bit unsure at the king's comment, I offered Kieran a chair. It was not that I was displeased to see her. I believed she had truly forgiven me for my deeds against her, and we were becoming close friends. Wander was the chief prophet of the creator in our land, but that made him a busy man, and I rarely saw him. Therefore, she had been vital in teaching me this new faith.

"Thank you, majesty," she replied as she sat.

"I see that you continue to view yourself as Sul's advocate. That is good," the queen interjected. I still found the age difference between the pair striking. I could only guess his prior wife had died, and it was not uncommon for a king to take a younger bride in that circumstance. "It will be good for others to note this development. Some are still leery of our former priest here."

"He is a changed man. The fervor with which he once served the gods is now directed against them. It is clear to me that Wander was correct all along. While I admit to my initial difficulty, I am now pleased with the decision to save his life."

"I am pleased to hear that," the king said, then turned to me. "How is your shoulder? I have been praying for it to be healed as well."

"I have too, majesty," I responded. "But that petition has not been granted. I continue to pray that the pain be removed, but I am resigned to the likelihood that it will not. It is my burden to bear. It is a constant reminder of my past and what a wretched man I am. However, it will not stop me from fighting to free Su'Meeryn from the pagans."

"Very good," Typheus continued. "Now, tell me, what do you make of all this?"

"All what, majesty?"

"Your past, your future, your healing. You are a unique man, Sul. I imagine nobody has ever experienced what you have. Amyon has been following the creator longer than any other kingdom in the lands. I was the first king to reject the gods after traders from across the northern sea brought their faith to my kingdom. I had always been skeptical of the gods, but I had been too much of a coward to voice my concerns before then."

I had to pause and consider his statement. This was all that had been on my mind since that day under the tree, but it was not easy to formulate my thoughts into words. So I decided to stall. "Forgive me, majesty, but it is strange to hear a king confess to cowardice."

Typheus smiled at my comment. "I am sure that is so," he said as his thin voice cracked. He took a moment to regain his strength before continuing. "Most certainly, I would never have said that out loud while

I was still a pagan. Personal vulnerability is not a character trait cherished by the gods. In our faith, honesty is championed, even if it puts oneself in an unfavorable position. I must say, even when I was younger and no longer a pagan, I still would not have admitted to it. But I am an old man now. Vanity does not concern me."

"I appreciate your words, majesty, but may I ask you a question? As I look about your hall, I see no gems or precious metals on display. It seems like jewels were pried out from your throne. Why?"

"You are a direct man, Sul. I like that, but I will allow my bride to respond."

Phillemy placed the cards she still held onto the table and rested her hand on her husband's wrist. "As I'm sure you have deduced, I am not Typheus' original wife. His first queen died in childbirth decades ago. He loved her so much that he vowed he would never marry again. But his children saw his unhappiness with not having a queen. They continued to prod him to remarry, and ten years ago, he acquiesced.

"Many people in the court did not view me favorably. They thought I just wanted to take advantage of an old man. Certainly, many women would relish the opportunity to be queen, but honestly, I was not one of them. When Typheus courted me, I decided I would marry him, as I knew my only intention was to serve him and Amyon. I requested that all the costly materials be removed from the hall. I told Typheus that we could use them to help those people less fortunate in his kingdom. Many of the nobles opposed that decision. They felt it cheapened the prestige of the kingdom, but I no longer care what they think of me."

"I see the king selected wisely," I said.

Phillemy grinned as she continued. "It seems you have deflected the king's question. He asked you your opinion regarding all that has happened, all that you experienced."

"My apologies. That was not my intention," I half lied. "it's just…well, it's not easy to put into words." As I hesitated, I looked at my three companions. They all gazed back at me with various expressions of sympathy. I was more comfortable accepting that sympathy from the king and queen, as I had done nothing directly to harm them, but I still felt a bit uncomfortable receiving compassion from Kieran.

"It is certainly difficult resigning oneself to the fact that you have lived your entire life for a falsehood: all those years wasted, squandered. All the people I've wronged weigh heavily on me. Every twinge of pain from my shoulder reminds me of them. So, in a way, this injury may be a blessing. It's not that I enjoy the pain or the memories of my sins, but what would it say if I ever forgot them? I'm already the worst of all sinners. I would be even worse if that memory evaporated, if that was even possible."

"You may be many things, Sul, but a stupid man you are not," the king croaked.

"He was considered perhaps the wisest man in all of Mephosh," said Kieran.

"I can see why," Typheus responded. "But what about your future?"

The comment left me a bit perplexed. "I'm not sure what you mean. We will leave for Su'Meeryn shortly. I will fight alongside Jaleph and do all I can to rid that kingdom of the pagan gods."

"Yes, yes, yes," the king continued. "But once the battle is over, if you survive, what will you do? You are no longer a priest. If you are not that, what are you?"

It was an interesting question. One I had not considered before, as my mind had been primarily focused on the upcoming task. Prior to this moment, my whole life had been mapped out. From a very young age, I had been groomed, along with Gallun, to be a priest and a warrior. Neither of those options appealed to me any longer. Yes, I would return to battle this one last time. I needed to make amends for the wrongs I had visited upon Su'Meeryn, but I did not want to kill anymore. In my pagan past, I relished the opportunity to inflict harm on anyone who opposed the gods. Now I only felt pity for those still mired in their pagan beliefs. What would I do after the battle? I had no idea.

"If we are victorious, I suppose I will leave that decision to Jaleph. He is the man who has suffered the most from me. His king is dead, all those other innocents dead. I will do as he commands."

Typheus nodded in satisfaction at my response. "Very good. I'm pleased we had this talk. Now, if the two of you will excuse us, the queen and I would like to finish our game."

"Thank you for your graciousness, majesty," I said as I stood from the table. "I appreciate it more than you could know." I strode from the hall with Kieran beside me. For some reason, I felt more at ease following that conversation than I had since my last battle. I am not sure why, but I noticed a great sense of calmness; a calmness that I had never experienced before.

"He's an interesting man," Kieran stated after the door to the hall closed behind us.

"Yes," I agreed.

"They seem to be a decent couple, despite…"

"He is a very old man."

"It gives me pleasure to see you coming to terms with your new life," Kieran said, changing the subject.

"I wish pleasure was the word I could use, but I understand your meaning. But let me ask you something, what should I make of you and Jaleph?"

"Is it that obvious?" she asked as we continued down the hallways of the castle.

"It is to me, as I have seen much of the two of you of late."

"He's a good man, a bit volatile, but a good man."

"I suppose many people would be volatile after all he's been through," I pointed out. Then another thought came to me. "With Teyon dead, and the fact that he had no family, I suppose Jaleph will be crowned king if we are victorious in securing Su'Meeryn."

"You are probably right."

"Then perhaps you would become queen. I've seen how Jaleph returns your affections."

"I hadn't thought of that," Kieran said as we reached my room.

I opened my door and looked back at her. I was not sure if I believed her statement, but it mattered not to me. At this moment, I could think of no better pair to become the new monarchs of Su'Meeryn. If part of her planned this, that was fine. Her compassion had been proven by the way she treated me. I vowed to myself that I would do all I could to see the pair crowned.

"It has been a pleasure spending time with you, Kieran. I truly hope that your desires are fulfilled. Now, please excuse me. I need to prepare myself for what is to come."

* * *

The next day I met with Jaleph and Pytr, Typheus' military commander. Pytr was a slender man with long, thin gray hair. A small headband kept his hair in place, and the emerald in the center of the band practically matched his green eyes. His face was cleanly shaved, and his necklace also sported a large emerald with a ruby on each side. A small emerald earring sat in each ear, and a clean, white shirt was visible under his dark green jacket. His pretentious attire was in stark contrast to the humble appearance of his king and queen. Due to his presentation, I felt an immediate disdain for him, but I figured I would spend some time with the man before passing my final judgment.

We met in the royal hall to plan the attack on Su'Meeryn. The king and queen were not present, but they allowed us to use the room, as it was the most secure in the kingdom. We wanted to take every precaution to avoid spying ears.

"As I have never been to Su'Meeryn, I will have to mostly defer to the two of you," Pytr began.

"The opening in the wall is to the south. If we attempt to circle the castle, that will give them more time to prepare," I stated.

"It hasn't been long, but I would expect your people have begun repairs on the wall," said Jaleph.

"I believe you are correct," I agreed. "Oziah is a capable man. He certainly thinks Su'Meeryn is fully in Lynna's hands, so he will have begun the work, but I doubt there has been much haste. With Teyon dead, he's not likely expecting an attack. Mephosh and the priesthood have no idea how widespread the faith is."

"So, what is our best course of action?" asked Pytr.

"Speed will be our ally," said Jaleph. "If we can move everyone fast enough, as we have planned, we will reach Su'Meeryn before they know we are coming."

"I am aware of that," Pytr answered sharply, "but how do we take the castle? We will have no siege engines to breach the north wall. If we bring them, we will be moving much slower, and certainly they will prepare."

"We have no choice but to circle the castle and attack from the south. They will know we are there, but we can't avoid that," I said. "We won't know how much progress they made in repairing the wall, but they cannot have gotten very far. We should be able to overwhelm them with our numbers. Unfortunately, this means it will be bloody for both sides." I wanted to point that out, as I would not underestimate my foe like the last time I attacked Su'Meeryn, but I did not want to stir that memory in Jaleph. "We need to get moving quickly. We need all our forces to strike out from Pathum before Oziah has more time to repair that wall."

Pytr's green eyes danced between us as he considered my words. "Very well. I will see to it that we are able to leave tomorrow. Do what you need to prepare yourselves, gentleman. We leave at first light."

"There is another matter," I continued. "Assuming we prevail, we have to consider what happens next. Lynna will not respond well to losing Su'Meeryn. She will most definitely launch a counterattack."

"Are you certain?" asked Jaleph. "If we do win, Mephosh will be weakened considerably. Despite past victories, Lynna will have lost many men."

"That is true, but Lynna is very rich. She has been collecting extra taxes from Su'Meeryn for a long time, and your treasury was emptied following the last battle."

"It still seems unlikely to me," Pytr interjected. "Surely your people will be weary of war."

"I know the queen well," I pointed out. "I've been one of her closest advisors for years. She is a smart and disciplined woman, but she is very self-conscious. She will not take well to being affronted. Rest assured, retaking Su'Meeryn will be her top priority. She will spare no expense."

"My king is committed to helping remove the pagans from Su'Meeryn," Pytr responded. "I cannot speak regarding what he will authorize following that. However, I will broach the subject with him."

"Thank you. I suppose that is all we can expect at the moment," I said.

As the three of us exited the hall, I was surprised by how different Pytr's personality was from his appearance. He was a man who clearly put much thought and effort into how he looked, but he also apparently was a man who knew his limitations. It was remarkable that Amyon's military leader would so easily defer to Jaleph and me regarding the assault. This was not a trait I was used to seeing in powerful men. It would be interesting to get to know him more.

Chapter 15

I SAT UPON MY HORSE WITH JALEPH AND KIERAN on my right and left. Jaleph had not been pleased when Kieran arrived and announced she would accompany us. Despite his many protests, she refused to stay behind. While she would not be able to participate in the attack, she said she would help treat the wounded. And, although Su'Meeryn was not her city, she said she would not stay here or ever return to Mephosh. I understood there was more to her decision than just the pagan religion and cruel memories of our home, and Jaleph eventually offered a knowing smile when it became clear she would not be dissuaded.

The sight of Wander riding up to us was a bit of a surprise to me. Whenever I asked about him, I was repeatedly told he was busy with other matters, so I had rarely seen him since the day of the storm. It was still strange to think of the man I had only known as a servant back in Mephosh as one of the most powerful men in the realm. He greeted the three of us, and his dark skin stood out against the entirety of the army waiting behind. In the past, I had occasionally questioned him about his homeland and how he had come to Mephosh. For whatever reason, he never wanted to talk about it.

"I see you have decided to join us," stated Jaleph.

"Yes, I initially wasn't sure if I should. However, after my prayers last night, I am compelled that it is what is required of me." Wander then cast a quizzical eye at Kieran, but he did not say anything more.

Our army was ready to proceed. We only awaited the arrival of Pytr. When he finally showed up, I had to stifle a laugh. Of the scores of men around me, he was the only one cleanly shaven. He sported a new headband, which displayed a sapphire stone that contrasted his green eyes. Instead of his emerald earrings, today he wore diamonds, and his necklace was now a string of pearls. His bright yellow coat would not remain as such once we started to ride. I assumed he felt his appearance before his men at this moment was more important than the beating the coat would take during the journey. If that is how he felt, I found it of no consequence. But I again noted the differences between this man and his king and queen, and it continued to baffle me.

"Gentlemen," Pytr began, "and my lady. Please excuse my tardiness. The royal couple wanted a brief word with me before we got underway."

"And what was the king's response?" Jaleph asked. "Will your army remain after the battle?"

"He would not commit one way or the other. I'm to assess the situation once the combat is concluded."

"It would be helpful if we knew what to expect," I said. "The coming battle will not be the end of the conflict if we are victorious."

"Yes, I'm sure that you would, but all I can tell you is what I have been instructed by my king."

"Either way, we have to liberate Su'Meeryn," Jaleph stated in an irritated tone as he fidgeted anxiously atop his mount.

"Agreed," said Wander. "We will take this one step at a time."

"That is not the best way to plan such things," I pointed out.

"No, but it is all we can do right now," Wander replied.

"Okay, all is now prepared. Let us start." Pytr signaled to his soldiers behind us and led the large group from under the castle gate. Once we were out in the open, Pytr picked up the pace. We wanted to reach Pathum as quickly as possible to meet up with the other armies.

We spurred our horses, and a light rain began to fall as we sped our way south.

***

Once the entire force was gathered, it was decided that Jaleph would be the leader of the army, since he knew Su'Meeryn better than anyone else. Most of the army had to camp outside the city as Pathum did not have enough open rooms to house the warriors from the three neighboring kingdoms. I had volunteered to stay with the rest of the men, but Jaleph ordered me to enter, as he wanted me to be a party to further deliberations.

Jaleph, Kieran, Wander, Pytr, and I sat in a small room in the castle as we discussed what we expected to happen the following day. The rain had continued throughout our journey to Pathum, but it was primarily a light drizzle, which had not slowed us down. If the rain did not increase in intensity, we would reach Su'Meeryn the following evening, and the attack would begin while some light still remained.

After much back-and-forth and some bickering, Pytr interjected, "As long as you agree, I suggest that we divide our forces once we reach the castle. We will circle from both sides, then meet at the breach in the wall. We will move faster that way."

"I suppose that is our best option," Jaleph answered.

"Very good. I'm not sure that we have much else to discuss. We do not know exactly what we will find when we arrive, but we should be able to overpower the city, assuming the hole remains," Pytr continued. "If you agree, sir, I will excuse myself to return to my men." Jaleph nodded, and Pytr rose from the table and left the room.

"His coat did not handle the trip well," Jaleph quipped once the door closed behind him.

Kieran chuckled briefly before being interrupted by Wander. "Do not be so quick to judge him, Jaleph. We spent much time together while in Amyon. He is a good and devout man, and I was assured that he is an excellent warrior."

"Pardon me," I interjected, "but I am struggling with understanding him. Typheus and Phillemy are very humble in their appearance. Why such an ostentatious appearance for a subordinate you claim is devout?"

Wander looked at me. "Why not? It is not something I would choose for myself, as I agree with how the king and queen present themselves. But If Pytr takes pleasure in his appearance, that is his choice. As I said, he's a good man."

I sensed a bit of irritation in Wander's voice, and I wanted to put him at ease. "Forgive me, I'm not questioning his character. This faith is new to me, and I am just trying to understand it."

Wander's face immediately softened. "No, please, I am the one who should apologize. My frustration was not directed at you." And his eyes immediately turned back to Jaleph.

"Do not preach at me, Wander," Jaleph barked. "My opinions are my own."

"You would do well to remember your place," Wander retorted. "You were put in charge of the army solely due to your knowledge of Su'Meeryn. Not everyone agreed with that decision, though."

"I don't care who agreed and who didn't. This is where we are now."

As the tension grew in the small room, Kieran stood and glanced at both men. She had known Wander for a while now and had clearly grown close to Jaleph. She did not want the situation to spiral out of control. "Please, this is a trying time for all of us. The combat will start soon enough, and while we expect to prevail, that is not a certainty. Much hinges on tomorrow in finally ridding the land of the pagan gods and restoring Su'Meeryn as an independent kingdom. Let's remember who the true enemies are. And let's remember that even if we are successful, there is no guarantee that we will all survive the violence."

Both men's expressions relaxed at Kieran's words. I understood far too well both of their passions, as I once had exhibited the same, even though my passion had been so misguided. The pressure of their different yet connected desires clearly brought stress upon them both.

After a few moments of silence, Wander spoke up. "How is your shoulder, Sul?"

"It is the same," I answered, "but I am unconcerned. I will be able to fight."

"How will you feel about fighting against your countrymen?" asked Jaleph.

"I do not look forward to it, but it is ultimately what is best for Mephosh. Once Mephosh stands alone, the belief in the gods should eventually dissolve and free the people from paganism."

"Is that all you care about?" Jaleph continued.

"No. I will do everything I can to make amends for the misdeeds I visited upon you and your city. There is little doubt that you will be crowned the new king of Su'Meeryn if we are successful. I am committed to making that happen, regardless of the cost."

"Then what?" Wander asked.

"I was asked that same question by Typheus. I don't know. That will be up to Jaleph." I looked at Jaleph, and he looked back at me. I could tell his expression was troubled, but beyond that, I could not read his emotion. It did not matter. The only thing I cared about has been freeing Su'Meeryn. What things I might do following the battle…well, I could not think on those now.

"We should all get some sleep," Kieran said. "It will be an early morning tomorrow."

As Jaleph and she rose, Wander motioned for me to stay. Before the pair left, Wander said, "My apologies if I was short with you, Jaleph. I look forward to riding together." Jaleph only nodded as he left.

"What may I do for you?" I asked when Wander and I were alone.

"We haven't had much opportunity to talk lately. I wanted to see how you are doing."

"As I said, my shoulder—"

"That is not what I mean. How are you handling your transition?"

"It's not easy, but I suppose it is going as well as can be expected," I answered.

"Please explain."

"I am fully devoted to your cause. I suppose I should say our cause. It's just that I remain haunted by my memories. Those thoughts and visions are never far from my mind."

"That is understandable. Though you may try to make amends for them, your past will always remain a part of you."

"That isn't very comforting."

"Do you want me to comfort you?" he asked.

"No, I suppose not," I said after a hesitation, but I was not sure I meant it. Yes, comfort would be nice, but was I worthy of that?

"I didn't think so. But I wanted to reassure you I remain confident we were correct in saving you. You have a vital role to play in what lies before us. Of that, I am convinced."

Wander's words helped soothe me somewhat. While I would never be able to erase my former deeds, I could be of some use to my new friends now. It felt reassuring to have a purpose again. One not directed by the lies of the false gods.

"Thank you, Wander," I said, gazing at his still-damaged face.

"Kieran was correct. We need to get some sleep. I will see you in the morning."

***

The combined warriors gathered outside Pathum at first light. It was an impressive sight. The army was huge, and I had never seen so many horses before. We even had horses for those who managed our supplies. Jaleph sat upon his steed, an image of utter confidence and determination with Kieran beside him. They emanated a royal appearance which I greatly approved of.

Pytr rode up next to me. He was dressed the same as the day before. He had clearly attempted to remove as much dirt and mud as possible from his garments without much success. However, his mood remained as pleasant as it had always been. With each new meeting, I started to like the man more and more.

As the sun broke the horizon, the sky displayed only a few thin clouds. The rain had ended, and it appeared we had been blessed with perfect weather for our trek to Su'Meeryn. Unfortunately, we all knew what awaited us upon our arrival.

With the light growing, Jaleph signaled, and our army began our journey to war. While I was anxious to do all I could to redeem myself, I was not looking forward to returning to the blood and death that loomed.

Chapter 16

SHADES OF CRIMSON FILLED THE SKY as the sun continued its progression to the horizon. The deepening hues of red were a portent of the blood that would soon be spilled. Not so long ago, I would have felt a sense of eager anticipation for the battle that was to come. Now I felt only dread. Dread and determination. I remained fixated on vanquishing the pagans from Su'Meeryn and establishing Jaleph as the new king, but the thought of killing again turned my stomach.

As we approached the city, we saw no signs that our army was expected. It appeared the plan had worked. Jaleph called out as the castle wall came into sight, and we all spurred our mounts. Dust and mud kicked up from the ground and swirled around the horses giving the impression of many small tornadoes.

Calls from the castle towers reached our ears: we had been spotted. Of course, this was anticipated, but so far, I was thankful that everything was proceeding as planned. With the height of the walls growing, Pytr veered his horse to the left, and half of the army followed him. Jaleph and I turned our mounts to the right and raced down the western side of the castle.

Arrows began to fall from the top of the walls as we sped on. As Jaleph and I were leading our column, I could not tell how many of the missiles found a target. Overhead I saw a few arrows flying up from our own archers. We assumed that our missiles would be even less successful than theirs, but they might serve as a distraction, if only for a short time.

As we reached the corner, we turned our horses to the left and raced to the breach in the wall. Within a few moments, we would know how much of the opening remained. Arrows continued to fly towards us as we reached our destination. To my surprise and delight, I saw a few stones had been added, but very little work had been done. Complacency is a malicious companion. As I had expected, it was clear neither Oziah nor Lynna were concerned an attack might be forthcoming.

Pytr's group reached the breach at the same time as mine, and since our horses would only get in the way now, we jumped from them, drew our weapons, and rushed forward. The castle's defenses were still forming as we raced through the opening.

We met the hastily formed defense, and the first clash of swords rang in my ears as the pain in my shoulder erupted. Even though I had anticipated it, it was still jarring. Jaleph fought next to me, and I noticed he had already dispatched two defenders. Ignoring my suffering, I swung my weapon again. The man who found himself as my opponent maintained a strong defense, but then I noticed a brief hesitation from him. Clearly, he recognized me, and that was the opening I needed. A quick flick of my wrist sent his sword twirling from his grip. He stared wide-eyed at me as I plunged my blade through his throat. Blood burst from the wound and his mouth as he collapsed before me, his eyes still wide.

Spinning about, I searched for my next victim. Two men rushed at me, both holding maces above their heads. I side-stepped the one to my left, dropped to one knee, and slashed his thigh. He cried in pain as he tumbled to the ground. I sprung to my feet, ready to face my other adversary, when I saw Pytr dash forward. The man had not spotted him, and Pytr's sword crashed down on his arm. Our opponent howled in agony as he dropped his mace. I deftly sliced his throat as Pytr finished off his companion.

I raised my gaze and beheld the beauty of the dusk sky juxtaposed against the carnage and death all around. I hated that I was once again embroiled in war and killing. I hated the person all those years of deceit had made me. My shoulder ached, and I once again felt like I was the most loathsome person who had ever lived. This musing lasted only a moment, as I had to return my attention to the battle.

We continued to push our way further into the city. The defense was growing and becoming more organized as the warriors from our combined forces flowed in. Arrows from the top of the walls continued their rain of death as the archers now found it much easier to locate their targets as our men had to slow to pass through the breach. Now that we held some ground, our archers turned back and launched their own barrage to the top of the wall.

I did not have time to gaze about further. My sword spun around me, leaving trails of blood flying in the air. With each blow, the pain in my shoulder increased, but I ignored it as much as possible. The cries of the dying surrounded me, and I tried to block them out the same as I did my pain.

My latest victim had fallen at my feet, his blood exploding in my face. I quickly wiped it away from my eyes, and I had a few seconds to take a couple deep breaths. The carnage everywhere was visible, even in the failing light, and it was sickening. Bodies lay askew all about the ground and appeared like islands in a scarlet sea. Some of the bodies still quivered as a light rain began to fall. To my right, I saw Pytr fighting off three men. I rushed to his aid as carefully as possible. I would be of no assistance if the worsening footing caused me to fall.

Pytr skillfully fought off the attack, and I was surprised at his prowess, which did not mesh with his pompous appearance. While he was holding his own against the men, he could not mount his own offense. Just as I reached the small group, I saw Pytr take a slicing blow off his left forearm. His blood began to join the muck that surrounded us. I heard a muted cry of pain, and I knew he would not survive much longer on his own.

Before the men could press their advantage, my sword pierced the spine of one of his attackers. Not allowing the other two any time to respond to this new threat, my blade was quickly out of the man's flesh and crashed down on the skull of the next. With the odds now in our favor, Pytr's sword pierced the heart of the third man. Pytr managed a quick nod of gratitude before he dashed off to find his next prey.

I took a second to glance back. Our men were still pouring through the breach, and some were climbing the walls to finish off the Su'Meeryn archers. I wondered if the defenders would surrender at this point, but they obviously thought they still had a chance to hold the castle.

Hearing the sound of an advance, I spun around in time to see two men rushing toward me. Despite the blood and filth that covered me, they both paused with expressions of recognition. That was a fatal mistake. I leapt at them and buried my sword in the abdomen of one. The other man recovered from his shock and swung. I pulled my dripping sword out and defended the blow. The blades crashed together as I felt a new wave of agony shoot down my shoulder into my fingertips. I grimaced in pain but stifled a cry from escaping my lips, not wanting my foe to realize my predicament. As I twisted to face him, my foot slipped on the blood and rain-soaked ground. I fell to one knee, and the man gave me an evil smile, thinking he had me. He clumsily struck down, but, despite my position, I deflected it and pushed my still throbbing shoulder into his waist. He slipped in the muck but did not fall. As he tried to regain his balance, I drove my sword into his left foot. He shrieked as his own sword fell from his hand. I tried to pull my blade out, but it was caught either in his foot or something hidden on the ground. Rather than struggle with it, I grabbed his weapon and rose to my feet. The last thing he saw was his own blade plunging into his face.

With those two dispatched, I searched about for my next victim. The first sight to register in my brain was Jaleph, surrounded by four men, one of them was the unmistakable shape of Oziah. Jaleph was covered in blood and gore, and he was fighting the men off as best he could, but I could see exhaustion threatening to overcome him. Even with his superior skill, he would not survive long if I did not arrive in time to intervene.

I reached the small group unnoticed just as Jaleph took a glancing blow to his head. I saw his eyes roll up as he collapsed. My commandeered blade took the first of the four in the side of the neck. He was dead before he hit the ground.

In that moment, all the pain totally evaporated from my body. I felt strong, and all my weariness had disappeared. My vision was completely clear despite the now late hour and the rain which still fell. The entire scene was illuminated as if the sun sat high in a cloudless sky. Oziah remained focused on Jaleph, but the other two men turned toward me. However, everything around me seemed to have slowed. The battle continued to rage, but every movement was at a snail's pace. Everything that is, except me.

As they approached, their movements were so sluggish it was almost comical. They were no threat to me. I was able to slay both effortlessly before they could even raise their weapons. Despite this altered state that I was in, I could not stop Oziah's blade from striking Jaleph. Fortunately, his foot skidded a bit on the slick ground, and his blade crashed down on Jaleph's shoulder instead of his head. The weapon sliced through Jaleph's skin, and I heard the cracking of bone. The arm went limp as Jaleph fell onto the crimson-stained ground. I knocked Oziah's sword from his hand, grabbed his left shoulder, spun him around then punched him in the face. My fist hit his nose, which exploded from the impact. He cried out in pain as his hands went to his face. When he realized who had defeated him, his eyes grew wide, and I saw traces of shock and anger from around his fingers.

I aimed my sword at his neck as my vision cleared, and everything was hazy again from the fading light and drizzle. The movement around me had returned to normal, and the pain in my arm returned.

"Sul?" Oziah cried. "What in the name of the gods are you doing?"

"It's over, Oziah. The castle is in our hands." I pushed him to the ground and pressed the tip of my blade against his throat. "You will surrender to us, or you will die."

"To us?" His confusion remained. He was certainly surprised to realize that I was alive and that I was fighting against him.

"All will be explained in time. Will you surrender, or do I have to kill you too?"

Oziah's body, which had been stiff with anger and confusion, sank into a state of resignation. I pulled him up, and we glanced about, my sword still tickling his skin. The battle continued around us, but it was clear the Su'Meeryn forces would not prevail. The defenders were being overwhelmed when Oziah called out for surrender. I also called for our warriors to cease their attack.

By the time the violence concluded, I waved two men over and ordered them to secure Oziah, and I rushed to Jaleph. In the fading light, no one else had noticed him. Kneeling down, I called for help. I saw that he was unconscious as I ripped off my shirt. The rain finally stopped while I wrapped my garment around his shoulder. The wound was deep, and I saw splinters of bone everywhere. While I had temporarily stopped the blood flow, I knew the wound was severe. Two others joined me as I searched for additional wounds, but I saw none other than a bruise on the side of his head. As the men gently lifted him, Jaleph's arm dangled at a sickening angle from his shoulder. I knew it would not be able to be saved. "Make sure it is amputated and cauterized quickly," I instructed as they took him away.

I now took the opportunity to examine my surroundings. The light in the sky was almost gone, but I saw the bodies lying askew everywhere. Some appeared to be in horrific embraces, and I could no longer make out the color of the blood in the dwindling light. I was thankful for that.

I then realized how exhausted I was. I had been sucking in deep breaths of air without even noticing it. I walked back to the castle wall and sat against it, trying to recover. The pain in my shoulder, though constant now, was more of a dull ache. I was grateful for that small mercy. Then I realized I was resting at the same spot I had with Gallun not so long ago. The irony almost made me laugh.

How many more men had I killed? I did not want to try to count. The thought made me sick. Despite my remorse, I felt different than I had in past conflicts. Normally I would have experienced a giddiness at this point. My arrogance and pride would have brought me pleasure. Now I felt no pleasure. I was disgusted by the death that surrounded me and that I had contributed to it. In the place of perverse bliss, I now felt a sense of resigned accomplishment. This was a task that had been necessary. Yes, difficult and unpleasant, but Su'Meeryn needed to be liberated to free the inhabitants from the unholy rule of the false gods.

With the light now gone, I dropped my head into my hands and began to cry. I wanted to be done with all this killing, but I knew I was not yet free. Lynna would not remain idle, and her rage would force her to attempt to retake Su'Meeryn. At least one more battle awaited me. Once more, I would be surrounded by carnage and death.

The tears continued to flow as exhaustion overtook me, but sleep arrived and relieved me of my misery.

Chapter 17

THE LIGHT OF THE NEW DAY, along with the sounds of movement all around, roused me from my slumber. I slowly rose from against the castle wall to a stiff back and still aching shoulder. The bodies had been removed from the courtyard, and I noticed billows of smoke outside the castle. The thought of the number of corpses necessary for the fires to still be burning was appalling. While the bodies were gone, the ground remained stained in blood. I glanced at my hands, and they were completely red, as I assumed the rest of my body was too.

I felt numb from the events of the previous evening. Would I ever be able to escape my past? And what of that transformation that I had experienced? What had overcome me? I never heard of anything like that before. Was this what Wander had foreseen? But then I wondered if I had only imagined it. Perhaps it had just been a trick of the mind due to exhaustion.

I wanted to ponder this further, but this was too much to consider at the moment. Now I needed to find out about Jaleph's state, and I wanted to find Pytr. Had he survived? And where had Oziah been taken to? Certainly, Lynna would hear the news soon if she had not already. Su'Meeryn needed to prepare for another attack. With the castle retaken, Pytr had not agreed to stay with his remaining warriors. And what of the soldiers from the other kingdoms? Yes, much work remained, but first, I had to clean myself. I needed to remove the blood and filth from my body before I could do anything else. I needed to cleanse myself.

Stares followed me as I made my way to the palace. I was not sure what I would find there, but I knew I would be able to bathe and secure unsoiled clothes. As I walked, I realized that I was not carrying a weapon. Although I was not expecting any difficulty, I felt almost naked without a sword. But I did not care. I relished this moment of not clutching a blade.

As I neared the palace, a few gawking people approached me. They thanked me for helping liberate them from Mephosh. When I acknowledged them, more mustered up their nerves, and soon I was surrounded. Men grasped my hands, and women patted me on my back, and, unfortunately, some of the pats found my shoulder. I masked the pain as best I could before I stopped, turned, and addressed the growing group.

"People of Su'Meeryn, yesterday was a tragic yet glorious day. Thanks to Jaleph, the city has been freed from the pagan grip of the gods. But rest assured more work is needed. Much will be asked of all of you in the coming days. Prepare yourselves and wait to hear from Jaleph."

The crowd roared at my words, and I was thankful they clearly did not recognize me from my prior visits to their city. "Now, please excuse me. I need to clean myself and attend to Jaleph." They roared again and started to disperse. I watched their faces and marveled at the fickleness of the citizens. Oziah had previously commented how he expected no strife upon becoming the new regent. Now they celebrated our victory. They must have been satisfied that the drought had ended, and they figured their taxes would decrease if they were no longer a vassal to Lynna. I suppose it was an understandable attitude. As I continued my walk to the palace, I was thankful to be alone again, if only for a short time.

***

I entered the royal hall, or what had been the royal hall in the prior days of the kings before Mephosh had conquered Su'Meeryn. Jaleph was stretched out on blankets, unconscious. His arm had already been removed, and Kieran knelt beside him. She wiped his forehead with a damp cloth, then tilted a mug above his mouth, letting a few drops of water fall to his lips. She smiled when she saw me enter.

Pytr stood next to the former throne, speaking with a few other men. He too was cleaned up but displayed none of the ostentatious garb I was accustomed to seeing. When he spotted me, he excused himself from his conversation and approached.

"The castle is secure, and from what I hear, most of the inhabitants are pleased to be rid of their conquerors," Pytr said.

"You and your men fought well," I said. "Jaleph and all the people of Su'Meeryn are indebted to you, as am I."

"We did what we were commanded by Typheus."

"Nevertheless, I am most thankful. What have you decided about staying? Given Jaleph's condition, we need someone to lead the army."

Pytr was obviously displeased with my comments. His demeanor made it clear he was anxious to return home. "This is not our battle anymore," he commented. "We agreed to help liberate Su'Meeryn, and that has been accomplished. Besides, we have already lost many men."

"If Mephosh retakes Su'Meeryn, the pagans will regain their foothold here, and all we have been through will have been for naught. If you allow Lynna's power to grow, what would be next? While the northern kingdoms have expelled the pagans, we don't know about the southern lands. We must limit Lynna's power now while she is at her weakest."

"This is no longer our battle," he repeated softly. "I don't want to see more of my men die."

My frustration was beginning to grow. I was confident Su'Meeryn would not be able to repel the certain forthcoming assault from Mephosh without the forces from Amyon and the other kingdoms. I took a moment to regain my composure, then motioned for Pytr to follow me to the chairs along the side of the hall.

"I don't want to see more death either," I began. "I have witnessed too much as it is. Typheus said you should examine the situation before making any decision. Surely you must see the importance of remaining."

Pytr sighed deeply as he looked about the hall. I followed his eyes to Jaleph before he turned back to me. "Of course I understand, but I have to think of Amyon first. How will staying help my king? I truly wish it was an easy decision, but it's not."

I then understood his dilemma. I had been viewing this ordeal strictly through my eyes and that of Su'Meeryn. Pytr had to also consider Amyon's interests; however, I remained convinced that both were aligned. I just needed to formulate the proper words to make him see. "I'm sure Jaleph and all of Su'Meeryn will be indebted to you if you stay. Lynna has plundered their treasury, so, as you know, Su'Meeryn is currently very poor. But there is more to owing a debt than just gold.

"And Lynna will certainly discover that Amyon fought against her. While I can't say that she will attack your kingdom, she will not forget the role you played."

"Sul, I like you. Obviously, we did not know each other when you were a pagan priest, so my judgment is not clouded by your past." He leaned back and placed his hands on his face, then ran them through his thin hair. "As Typheus left it to my discretion, I will remain. For now. I'll send a couple couriers back home to advise him of our situation. We will stay unless I receive word otherwise. If orders come back for us to leave, that is exactly what we will do."

"I could ask for nothing more."

"You are a man gifted with words," Pytr said as we saw Kieran stand and approach us.

"He is waking," she said.

We followed her back to where Jaleph rested on the ground, with Wander beside him. Jaleph's eyes were open, and his face was contorted in pain. He reached his remaining hand to where his other shoulder had been, and his painful countenance morphed to despair when he realized his arm was gone. Kieran sat next to him and tenderly stroked his forehead. "You are alive, and the city is secure. We won," she said softly.

"Help me up," Jaleph said weakly.

Wander knelt too, and he and Kieran assisted Jaleph to his feet. He winced again, and his knees nearly buckled. Then his gaze fell on me, and I saw that any goodwill I had gained in Jaleph's mind had evaporated. I could tell exactly what he was thinking: his new hardship was my fault. If it wasn't for my previous actions, Su'Meeryn would not be in this position, and he would still have his arm.

"Jaleph," Wander quickly stated, apparently seeing the same development that I did. "Sul is here to see how you are doing. We all owe him a debt. He fought off Oziah and a handful of others single-handedly and saved your life."

"How would you know that?" I asked. I was not aware anyone had seen what occurred in the failing light.

"I saw much," was his cryptic response.

Jaleph grunted at Wander's words, then grimaced in pain while absently reaching for his missing arm again. He glanced back at Kieran and asked her to help him from the room.

"It is unfortunate that Jaleph suffered such a devastating wound," Wander continued once Kieran and Jaleph were gone. "But he is still the best choice to be the new king."

"I care not who is selected to rule Su'Meeryn," Pytr responded, "but Jaleph has a short temper. I am not certain that I agree with you."

"At times, that is true, but Kieran will soften his moods," replied Wander. "They are both true believers, and Kieran's faith is even stronger than his. He will do fine once this crisis is past. I would prefer the new king present a stronger image to his people, but they will see how much he has sacrificed for them. He will be well received."

"I am certain that the crisis is not over," I pointed out.

Wander turned to me and gently placed his hands on my shoulders. I blinked in anticipation, but his light touch caused me no pain. "I agree, Sul. You were instrumental in the liberating of Su'Meeryn, and I am convinced you will serve an even greater purpose in the coming days."

"I'm not sure your faith in me is deserved."

With a warm smile, Wander responded, "None of us deserve anything, my friend."

"If you two will excuse me," Pytr interjected with an aggravated tone, "I will go now and make myself useful while I am still here. Since you are convinced Mephosh will attack again, someone should see to the defense."

"You are right," said Wander. "While you do that, I will meet with the nobles to prepare for the coronation of Jaleph."

As both men exited, I was left standing by myself in the hall. I wanted to work with Pytr in preparing the defense, but I had a different task I needed to complete first.

***

With a wary eye, the guard unlocked the cell door. "Are you certain you are safe?" he asked.

"I will be fine," I responded. After a moment, I continued. "But keep close, just in case."

Oziah stood as I entered the cell. "What are you doing here?" he sneered.

"I wanted to see you. Are you being treated well?"

He laughed at my words, then sat back on the ground. "We all thought you were dead, but then I find you alive. Alive and fighting with the enemy."

"They are not the enemy."

"How can you say that?" he spat. His ire toward me practically seeped out from his pores.

I stared at my friend. Yes, I still considered him a friend, even if he no longer returned the sentiment. How could I explain to him what I had experienced? Since the day my sight returned, I had only been surrounded by believers in the creator. How could I explain myself to someone who had believed in the gods his whole life, a person who believed I had wronged him?

"We have known each other a long time. You know me to be an honest man, Oziah. I am no longer a priest. I've come to realize that the gods are nothing more than a fable, a myth." I had expected Oziah to respond angrily to my words, so his silence surprised me. "Those that I had once called heretics, I realize now they hold the truth. I was the one who lived a lie my entire life."

"Sul, as you know, I was never much of a religious man. I acted in ways that were required of me. I care little for the gods and even less regarding this creator. Any belief I professed in the gods was a facade. My life is in service of my queen and our realm. Be a priest, don't be a priest. I don't care. But what you are is a traitor."

"Yes, I understand that you feel that way, but honestly, I do not view myself as such. I love our home, and I love our queen. The last thing I wanted to see was more blood spilled, but it was, unfortunately, necessary."

"Necessary?" he barked, "I will never agree with you on that. You raised your sword against your own countrymen. You killed them."

Oziah glared at me with a look of both disgust and disappointment. "I have done far worse than that, and I am reminded of it every day. I have beaten people I now call friends. I slaughtered the innocent. Yet, those acts didn't bother you."

"You did what was needed. My approval of those actions was not necessary."

I searched my mind, trying to find the words that would make him understand. "How long did we all pray to the gods to end the drought? As you know, it was to no avail."

"The drought is over," Oziah responded.

"It is, but it had nothing to do with the gods. After I killed Teyon, I was struck down by Jaleph. As you know, it was thought I was dead. Wander saved my life, but the blow I suffered blinded me. When we were in Amyon, Wander took me out into the wilderness. He knew exactly when the rain would come, and at that very moment, my sight was restored. The gods did not bring this about. It was the creator. It was then I knew my whole life had been dedicated to a lie, and I felt the guilt of all my past deeds."

"That is a nice story you tell, Sul. But how do I know it is anything more than that?"

"As I said, you are my friend, and you know I am not a liar. Think to yourself, why else would I be doing what I'm doing? You knew that I was the most devout man in all of Mephosh, perhaps the entire land. Why else would the man standing before you have renounced his entire life?"

I could see Oziah struggling for a retort, but no words came. Eventually, he responded, "What are you going to do when Lynna attacks again? We both know she will not stand for this. You raised your sword against me. Will you do the same to Gallun?"

His words struck me hard. I knew that I would have to fight my countrymen at least one more time. But the thought that I might need to face off against my closest friend had never crossed my mind.

"I do not enjoy any of this, Oziah. It is a tremendous burden I bear, but we must rid the land of these pagan false gods. That is of the utmost importance. I am committed to that. I will do whatever is necessary."

"Well, your zealousness certainly hasn't changed."

"Please, Oziah, ponder my words. Think of what I have said. Think of Wander and Kieran."

"Kieran? I had been told that Wander is part of this, but how is she involved?"

"She has been educating me in my new faith, and she will likely be the new queen of Su'Meeryn, but I don't have time now. I will come back when we can talk further."

Oziah snorted at my statement. "You are a traitor, Sul, and I have no interest in talking to you again."

His words were expected, but they still hurt. It seemed everyone close to me, I had wronged in one way or another. "Oziah, I am the worst of all men. I don't need to be reminded of that. But perhaps your opinion will change, as has many others. I will leave you to yourself, but I will make sure you are treated well."

"Thank you," Oziah responded sarcastically.

As I left the cell, I was not sure how I felt about the exchange. I certainly did not expect him to believe anything I told him, but I knew I had to try. I had to explain myself to my friend.

While leaving the dungeons, my shoulder started to ache again. I merely shook my head as I sought out Pytr. I needed to do all I could to prepare Su'Meeryn for what was to come. The thought of my friend sitting in a cell got me thinking of the other friend I might have to engage in battle very soon. Would this physical and emotional suffering never end? But I knew I deserved no respite. I would have to live with these consequences all of my days.

Chapter 18

WANDER HAD WORKED QUICKLY, and all the nobles agreed that Jaleph should be the new king. His courage and sacrifice were unmatched in all of Su'Meeryn, and he had been a close friend of Teyon. The one stipulation they requested was that he be married before the coronation. They did not want any squabbling amongst themselves as to who would be his queen. Certainly it would have been an advantage to marry off one of their daughters to the new king, but I assumed that Wander had much to do with the decision, as nobles are not often known for their selfless deeds. However, with all that Su'Meeryn had been through and what was coming, nobody wanted to add additional strife to the fledgling kingdom.

Early the following day, the nobles gathered, and Wander presided over the marriage of Kieran and Jaleph. The soon-to-be king still looked feeble and weak, the pain clearly visible on his face. The couple's garb was unspectacular, and Jaleph looked awkward in a brown leather coat with only one arm. But he appeared pleased enough during the rituals, except when he spotted me. At those times, his angry glares returned.

In contrast, Kieran's beauty beamed. She made a stunning bride even with her scar and maimed ear. Despite Jaleph's increasing discomfort throughout the ceremony, all who were present celebrated at the conclusion. When the marriage festivities ended, the couple quickly departed so Jaleph could rest.

It had been decided that Jaleph would be crowned the next morning when everyone hoped he would appear a bit stronger. It was one thing for him to look feeble at his wedding, but his coronation was another matter. Pytr and I excused ourselves and headed to the castle wall to check on the work being done.

As we walked down the street, I had to suppress a chuckle at Pytr's appearance. He wore an orange shirt with bright blue pants. A thick necklace dangled down his chest, and a ruby sparkled in the morning sun. Huge earrings hung from each ear, and I noticed cosmetics on his clean-shaven face. I wondered where he found all these items, but I had no desire to ask him. He remained an enigma to me. His garb was a striking contrast to the humble appearance of his king and queen. However, despite his look, I had seen his skill as a warrior during the battle, and the more I talked with him, the more I liked him.

"I want to thank you again for staying," I said to him.

"We serve where we are needed," he responded.

"Yes, but you were not obligated to remain, so I want you to know it is appreciated."

"Thank you, Sul. Tell me, how are you managing all this change?"

I pondered his words, along with the fact that he was not the first to ask me such a question. But there was something about his manner that drew me to him. "It is difficult," I answered honestly. "Seeing Jaleph's disdain is hard, but it's expected."

"I noticed as well."

"My life… It's like it has started over, that I'm a new person. I wish it was in fact true, but my memories remind me otherwise."

Pytr clutched my wrist and stopped us. "I see how hard all of this is for you, and I wish I had some advice to give. While I am a follower, I would not define myself as extremely reverent. All I can say is to focus on the task ahead. With Jaleph's injury, we will need you even more than when we took the castle."

"I find these expectations of me very unnerving." However, the comment brought me back to that short time of transformation on the battlefield, and I again pondered if that was what Wander had foreseen for me.

"We all have our roles to play, Sul, our tasks to fulfill. All we can do is be true to them."

His statement soothed me somewhat. I greatly appreciated how Kieran and Wander had embraced me, but this was the first time I contemplated that I might actually have something to offer, that my life may, in fact, have value. "Thank you, Pytr. Your words have helped tremendously." He grinned at me as we continued on our way. Yet as we started to walk, the pain in my shoulder returned along with all my regret, causing my mood to sour again.

When we reached the breach in the wall, we found scores of men and women working hard, dragging all manner of wood and debris they could find to fill the hole. Being that Su'Meeryn was situated in the middle of the Eusutal Plains, there were no trees nearby to cut down and transport to the castle. I figured we had a week at most to prepare for the onslaught, so we would not be able to fully seal the wall. But we would certainly be able to hamper the progress of the enemy, though.

The spiked logs that had impeded our initial attack had been chopped up at Oziah's order to fill the previously dug pits. We needed to think of a new means of defense. The nets that had been used were effective, even though they did not last long, but Gallun would be wary of those prior traps. We would need to think of something different. I told Pytr of that battle as we discussed various ways to hinder the forthcoming attack. While we talked, we spotted one of our scouts racing on his horse to the city. We stopped our conversation and waited for the man to arrive.

When he reached the wall, he jumped from his horse and started to climb through the work being done. He looked annoyed when we stopped him, but then he recognized Pytr and apologized.

"Report," Pytr commanded.

"The army is already heading toward us," he responded.

"How can that be?" I asked. "They would not have had time to organize."

"They are not fully organized, but they are sending siege engines north. The army is still gathering and just beginning to follow the catapults and towers. They are getting everything moving as quickly as possible. I estimate they will arrive in about six days."

"Thank you," Pytr said and dismissed the man. "This is troubling."

I was distraught to hear the news, but I probably should have expected it. Gallun was no fool. If they could not reach Su'Meeryn in short order, the soundest plan would be to bring the heavy equipment. He would be far more careful than the last time he attacked Su'Meeryn.

"At least we know what we are up against," I pointed out. "Now we just need to plan accordingly."

***

We all stood in the courtyard under a crisp blue morning sky in front of the nobles, with many of the townspeople behind them. A brisk wind blew, which seemed to amplify the excitement that was buzzing in the air. Jaleph wore a maroon robe with a golden cord around his neck and hanging down his torso. The absence of his left arm subtracted from the image, but he still looked fairly regal. His face was clean-shaven, and another golden cord was wrapped around his waist. He still appeared to be frail and in pain but not as bad as the previous day. Atop his head sat a circlet of green leaves.

Wander, who stood beside him, sported a black cloak with a silver belt as the only adornment. Kieran was on his other side. She wore a yellow dress with maroon etchings. A high collar covered the sides of her face, which I guessed was intended to hide her scar and ear. The large diamond on her necklace sparkled in the morning sun, as did her jeweled headband. Light cosmetics were barely visible on her face. She looked as beautiful as she did prior to the beating. For some reason, she asked that I stand beside her. My amazement at her affection for me remained.

As the chief of the nobles approached, Jaleph's posture straightened, and I was pleased to see he did look somewhat stronger for the ceremony.

"Jaleph," the man began. "Su'Meeryn is free from the rule of Lynna and Mephosh, but we find ourselves with no king. Teyon is dead, and he had no heirs. No one remains from his royal line. You served Teyon and Su'Meeryn for many years, and your courage and sacrifice in the recent troubles are known by all. As the appointed speaker for all the nobles, it is with pleasure that I announce we unanimously agree that there is no better choice for our new sovereign than you." He stopped and motioned for a servant to approach.

The woman carried a red pillow with a large crown of gold and silver. As she reached Jaleph, he bowed his head, and she removed his circlet and replaced it with the crown. She placed the circlet on the pillow and returned to the gathering. She handed the pillow to another servant, then was given a second one of yellows and blues. The queen's crown rested on that pillow, and the woman repeated the ritual with Kieran.

When the brief ceremony concluded, the man turned to the crowd. "I now present to you, Jaleph the first, the new king of Su'Meeryn, and his lovely wife, the queen Kieran."

The crowd erupted in applause, and I had to wipe a tear from my eye. These two that I had so wronged now ruled the kingdom of Su'Meeryn. However, the rule would be extremely short-lived if we were not able to stop Gallun and the impending assault from Mephosh.

Jaleph raised his arm, and the crowd slowly quieted. "My people, I humbly accept this honor you have bestowed upon me." His tone was stronger than I expected, but I sensed him masking an undertone of pain. "This is a position I never aspired to. Teyon was my king and my friend, and I wanted nothing more than to serve him for the rest of our lives. But as we have seen, situations change. I pledge to serve Su'Meeryn to the best of my abilities, whatever they may be now." He motioned to his missing arm, and nervous laughter arose from the mass of people. "As we all know, the threat is not over. Mephosh is advancing north to attempt to retake our lands. My vow is that as long as I remain alive, we will not be subjected to them again!" The crowd roared at his words.

When he continued, his voice began to weaken. "We have much to prepare. The next few days will be trying for us all, but once we are victorious, we will have time to rest and celebrate. For now, complete the tasks that you are assigned and know that your king will be working alongside you all as best I can."

The multitude cried in approval; banners were waved, and colored balls of thread were hurled into the air. As the threads unwound, they created the appearance of a myriad of small rainbows filling the sky. Eventually, the people filed away, and our small group was alone. Wander hugged Jaleph and Kieran. "Now, let's find Pytr," he said. "We need to finalize our plans for our defense."

***

Wander, Pytr, Jaleph, Kieran, and I sat together in Jaleph's small home. As his possessions had not yet been transferred to the castle, Jaleph did not feel comfortable meeting there. The activities of the day had made him weaker than he had been during the coronation and had increased his pain. So, he wanted to gather somewhere private and familiar.

We were all discussing plans to defend the castle, traps that could be set, and ways to slow down the army. I cautioned the others not to underestimate Gallun. We had taken the defense of Su'Meeryn for granted during the last attack, and Gallun would not make that mistake again. "He may be impulsive," I said, "but he is not stupid."

"Sul is correct," Wander stated. "I know Gallun too. Not as well as Sul does, but I do know he's a competent warrior. We need to think unconventionally."

"We have time to prepare," Pytr pointed out, "so we must take advantage of that. We must set traps this Gallun is unfamiliar with."

"I am not a warrior," stated Wander, "but I do know we need to try something unexpected. Something Gallun cannot anticipate."

"What do you propose?" Jaleph asked.

"Gentlemen, if I may interject," Kieran said. "We still have most of the horses from our attack. With the losses suffered from the battle, we can certainly mount our entire army. While the drought is over, the food supplies have not been completely restocked. Su'Meeryn could not withstand a prolonged siege if that were to happen. Why don't we ride out and intercept them? Gallun will not be expecting us to attack him."

We all sat silently for a moment, contemplating her words. "I agree with Kieran," I eventually said, annoyed that I had not thought of the plan myself. "I think her plan gives us our best chance of success."

After a bit more discussion, it was decided to proceed with the queen's idea. We would gather our supplies, then ride out at first light.

"And I will accompany you," Jaleph said.

"If I may, I don't think that's a good idea," Wander said.

"I cannot just sit back while you all fight for Su'Meeryn. I doubt I'll be of any assistance, but I will join the expedition."

"As will I," said Kieran.

I was not comfortable with either of them coming along, but it was clear their minds would not be changed. Once again, I was not looking forward to going into battle. More death awaited me, and I prayed this would be the last time. What would become of me after the next few days, I did not know, but I sensed my struggles were coming to a conclusion.

We all stood, and I felt that all-too-familiar ache from my shoulder. I watched as Kieran placed her arm around Jaleph's waist and helped him to his bed. The king needed to rest, and the image of his missing arm still haunted me. Yes, I was not the one who struck the blow, and I did save his life, but was I the one who had allowed this all to happen? Would Lynna have reacted differently if I had counseled her toward another path? The more I pondered the past, the more my pain increased. Would I ever be free of my memories? Even if we were victorious, could the blood that would be spilled wash away my sins?

I could not answer my own questions, but my vow to Jaleph and Kieran remained. Yes, they were now the rulers of Su'Meeryn, but that would not last if we lost the forthcoming battle.

I would worry about my personal demons later. Now, all I could focus on was defeating my closest friend.

Chapter 19

A TRAIL OF DUST FOLLOWED OUR ARMY as we raced through the Eusutal Plains. We had made only one brief stop for a short lunch and to rest the horses. A quick check of Jaleph found him weary, but he was managing the journey as best as could be expected. Kieran was tending to him, and I was still not pleased that they had come. I wanted to ask them to return to Su'Meeryn, but I knew that would be fruitless, so I just wished them well prior to relieving myself and remounting my steed.

As the sun started to make its way towards the western horizon, we stopped on a small rise and caught the first sight of our quarry. I glanced at Pytr, and the two of us examined the area as Wander brought his horse up to us.

A number of cavalry led the group, and I knew Gallun would be among them. The infantry followed, and we caught a glimpse of the catapults and siege towers in the rear. Behind that would come the supplies.

"How do you plan to proceed?" Wander asked.

Across the distance, we heard a cry from our foes. We had been spotted. That was not overly concerning, as we knew we would not be able to strike them with surprise. Pytr gazed about before turning to me. He wore plain garb for the coming conflict, but he still sported earrings and some light cosmetics. For the first time I had seen, he displayed some stubble on his face, which seemed confused by the vision before us. He might be a skilled fighter, but he obviously was not much of a tactician.

I stared at the enemy for a few seconds, considering our options. I had been contemplating a plan of attack during the journey, but I wanted to catch sight of our foe prior to making a final decision. "We charge straight in. They won't be expecting a wedge assault. We should be able to split their forces."

"But won't we be surrounded?" asked Pytr.

"We will have the speed. They won't be able to surround us and will be in disarray. If they are unable to organize, we shouldn't meet an appropriate defense."

"That sounds reasonable to me," Wander agreed. "I will leave it to you two warriors to work out. If you will excuse me, I will return to Kieran and the king. I will be in prayer for all of you."

As Wander rode off, I turned to my companion. "You have become a good friend over the short time I've known you. I will admit I misjudged you the first time we met."

"You are not the first person to tell me that," Pytr responded with a smile.

"I hope to find you alive when this is all over, but I must ask you. Why the attire?"

Pytr chuckled at my question. "I am a faithful man, Sul. Not as pious as Typheus and Phillemy, but devout nonetheless. I like to dress well, and if it doesn't hurt anybody, why not?"

"Dressing well is one thing, but…"

Pytr laughed again. "You find me somewhat…outlandish? That is purposeful. I find it throws people off when they meet me. It did you, didn't it? I like to be underestimated. I believe it gives me an edge. And as the military leader of Amyon, I am willing to take any edge I can get."

Now it was my turn to chuckle. "I don't think I would operate in such a manner, but I give you credit; you are fully committed to your principle. I hope we have many days ahead of us to discuss these things."

"As do I, my friend. I would be happy to host you in Amyon."

"Well, now that those pleasantries have been addressed, I suggest we get to it. We should delay no further," I stated.

"Agreed, we have hesitated long enough." With that, he raised his sword and signaled the wedge assault. The calls echoed behind us as the vanguard spurred their horses and charged forward. Pytr gave me one more look before taking off after them. I glanced up to the sky, offered my own brief prayer, then followed.

The warriors from Mephosh scurried about as our horses charged down on them. I was pleased with my decision as I saw confusion in their ranks as the first weapons met. The clamor of battle once again engulfed me. The sound of blades meeting reached my ears, along with a cacophony of orders being barked out. Then I heard the first cries of the wounded and the dying. I swung my sword and drove those sounds away, as I did the pain that burst in my shoulder.

We had penetrated the cavalry line and rushed towards the infantry. My sword swung in every direction. Droplets of blood permeated the air like a gruesome rainfall. I was sickened to be in this position again, but I had to push that feeling away as well. I had known this was coming, and I would deal with the ramifications later. That was if I survived. For now, I needed to accomplish my task.

Everywhere I looked, horses dashed about. Any semblance of an orderly attack had vanished. Our riders' weapons struck everywhere. Men fell to the ground, and some were trampled. Defenders fought back as best they could. Some targeted our steeds, and many of the horses fell victim, dragging their riders down with them.

Amidst the chaos, it was impossible to tell how the battle was progressing. It appeared that my plan for the frontal assault was working, but I could not discern which side was experiencing the heavier losses.

I continued to swing my blade at the scores of enemies. I missed often, but when my weapon did find a strike, I was unsure if the blade found flesh or if it had been deflected. Though I was a superior warrior, I rarely trained on horseback, so this was another oversight I cursed myself for.

While I was not as skilled on the horse, it was certainly an advantage against most of those I faced. I targeted my next prey, a grizzled warrior with his sword out, pointing toward me. I spurred my steed and charged at him. He braced for the impact, but as I approached, he stepped to his left, getting ready to swing. Unfortunately for him, I had anticipated that maneuver. At the last moment, I veered my horse to my right and barreled into him. My horse's flank struck his right shoulder and sent him spinning in the air. As he landed, I quickly turned my horse about. The man lay stunned on the ground. I reached him, and my horse reared up. I brought its hooves down onto his head. His skull cracked under the impact like the shell of a nut.

I pulled on my mount's reins to spin it back into the battle, but it did not move. I pulled again but still nothing. Confused, I glanced about and saw a handful of arrows jutting from its hide. The beast's legs buckled, and I knew I needed to dismount as rapidly as possible. If the animal fell and pinned me, I would be a dead man. I stood in the stirrups and sprung from its back just as it fell. I landed on the ground on my right side. I pushed myself up as quickly as possible as a new wave of pain exploded in my arm. I cried out while jumping to my feet. The pain was so severe that I retched, but I had to see what was around me. If I hesitated too long, I likely would not survive.

I managed to bury the pain, but I then realized that I had lost my sword in the tumble from my dying steed. Before I could search for one on the ground, two men approached. They were not mercenaries but warriors from Mephosh. As during the attack on Su'Meeryn, when they recognized me, they hesitated. Here was one of the most powerful men of Mephosh—a priest of the gods, whom they thought was dead, facing off against them. As I had experienced in the last battle, their hesitation was their undoing.

Prior to regaining their wits, I pounced, I leaped at the first man, and my elbow struck his throat. I heard him gasp for air as he doubled over. The second man had his sword raised. He was left-handed, and my right hand grabbed his left wrist. My agony returned, but it almost did not register in my brain. With my left hand, I punched him in the face, then I kneed him in the groin.

I knew his companion would recover soon, so I had to dispatch him quickly. He tried to shake off his own pain and pull free from my grip. His right hand grasped at mine and tried to pry it away. I punched him again, then twisted my body. I felt him loosen his grip on the sword hilt, and as he did, I yanked it away with my left hand. With it now free, I pushed it up with all my might through his chin and pierced his brain.

As I pulled the blade free, I saw that his companion had recovered enough for a counterattack. He must have lost his weapon too as he decided to wrap his arms around me and attempted to wrestle me to the ground. My arms were pinned, so the commandeered sword was useless. He was strong, and I was in a dire position as I could not free myself. I stomped down on his foot. I noticed him wince, but his grip did not loosen. The more he tightened, the more my arm cried in misery.

The pain was becoming too much. I retched again. The man said something, but I could not make it out. I was drowning in my pain. I tried to stomp on his foot a second time, but I had no idea whether I was successful. I knew I only had a moment to break loose. Otherwise, this was where I would die.

In one desperate move, I used what energy I had left to propel myself in the direction that he was pushing. He had not expected that move, and we fell to the ground. As we landed, his grip loosened, and I was able to roll us over so that I was on top of him. His grasp was broken. My arms were now free, and I realized I still held the captured weapon as I managed to flip over. He bellowed in disbelief as the blade punctured his chest. But then the pain in my shoulder overwhelmed me.

I screamed as my hands let the sword loose, and I fell beside him. The agony was too severe, and my arm would not move. I tried to stand, but there was no strength in my body. The blood was pouring from my last victim and drenched me in a sickening warmth. That warmth was almost welcomed. I hoped it might revive me, but it did not. I could not continue. I felt complete fatigue, and I was certain that my lungs were bruised. I was unable to recover and could not take a deep breath. The pain and exhaustion were too much. Survival appeared impossible. I was certain an adversary would find me in this helpless condition and drive a sword through my heart. I practically relished that forthcoming moment as it would at least end all my suffering. This seemed the most appropriate place for me to die: in battle between my former homeland and my new life.

Just as I resigned myself to my fate, all my agony disappeared. Exactly as had occurred in Su'Meeryn, I saw clearly in what was now the fading light. I stood, energized, and everything around me appeared to be moving at half speed, if not less. I pulled the sword from my victim's body and rushed back into the fray.

Opponents came at me, but their sluggish movements were now comical. I foresaw their every attack, and I easily dispatched them all.

Nobody could touch me. My sword seemed to be pulling me forward, bringing death to all enemies it spotted. The killing became so easy that I almost forgot what I was doing. As more of my foes were vanquished, the joy of the kill from my past life threatened to engulf me. I pushed that sense away as I reminded myself that this conflict was a necessity. Su'Meeryn was not planning an attack on Mephosh. It was the other way around. But did that matter? For the moment, I did not care.

I continued to cut my way through the battle. I saw that the sun was setting, but still, everything was as bright to me as a cloudless afternoon day. Three men approached with evil grins on their faces. They had the numbers and figured they would easily rid themselves of my menace. Those foolish grins would disappear soon enough.

What had overcome me on those two occasions, I do not know, but even three well-armed and well-trained men were no match for me now. Their movements were so slow that I disarmed the first two before they realized what was happening. As the third prepared to strike, I easily flicked my blade across his throat. Before he could even collapse, I spun on the other two. My sword crushed the skull of one, then split the stomach of the other. It was all too easy.

Scores of the enemy fell to my sword. It did not matter how many I faced off against. Their numbers were meaningless. Everything moved so deliberately that nothing was a threat. I lost count of the number of men that I killed. Once again, I was soaked in blood, and this time I knew none of it was mine.

I felt no pain in my shoulder despite the innumerable times I swung my blade, and I never tired. Nothing was able to stop me. I brought death with every passing second. But then, as if in answer to my own hubris, my vision darkened, and all my pain returned. But this time, the ache was not only in my shoulder. I felt a new pain in my left calf. I glanced down and noticed an arrow at my foot. Thankfully it had not entered my leg, but it had sliced the skin. I saw a fresh flow of blood, and everything now moved as normal. I found that I could at least breathe easily, but I had lost that otherworldly advantage.

The battle raged on before me. I caught a glimpse of Pytr and was grateful that he still lived. His sword whirled about him in what almost appeared to be a graceful dance. As everyone on the battlefield was covered in blood, I could not tell if Pytr had suffered any injuries. He moved in a way that appeared unhindered, which was good to see.

I could stand there no longer, the combat was drifting back toward me, and I needed to engage. I swung my weapon, and my pain multiplied as it was blocked. I stepped forward and struck again. Now the pain in my calf matched my shoulder. I gritted my teeth as I pressed on. The aching remained, but I kept it at bay.

As I pushed my attack, my lungs managed to suck in air, but I still felt the bruising in my chest. How I was able to continue, I do not know. While I felt all my suffering, it did not hinder me. I knew that my misery was there, but it was as if it had been separated from me, like a shadow.

I turned to find my next opponent. He was skilled, but he was no match for me. I quickly disarmed him. As his sword rattled to the ground, he cried out and jumped at me. I kicked my knee up to his hip, pushing him to the side. As he fell, my blade cracked the back of his head.

Two more men collapsed before me, then I heard my name called out from amidst the bedlam. Looking about, I heard it called again.

From out of the chaos, I saw Gallun emerge. "Sul, it is you!" he cried. He rushed at me with an expression of disgust and rage mixed with the filth covering his skin. His blade dripped fresh blood, as if it was crying crimson tears.

Our swords met with a ferocious crash. He struck out again, "I hadn't believed it." His face contorted into fury with the realization. Obviously, he had heard that I was alive and fighting with the enemy, but he must have thought that they were only sick rumors until the evidence stared him in the face.

"Surrender," I commanded as I fought off his blows. "Look about. Your army is being overwhelmed."

He continued his attack. "You know I can't do that." His rage remained. Despite the now low light, it was clear that we were winning. I saw that our forces had pushed the Mephosh army back towards the siege engines. But the look of betrayal on Gallun's face was clear. He would never stop until the traitor who had been like a brother to him was dead.

We continued to trade blows, but fatigue was setting in. My pain remained, but still, it seemed separated from my body. Gallun knew he was outmatched, but he would not stop. Each blow became wilder and more reckless as he knew he would not be besting me on this day. He then launched a desperate, lunging attack, but I had been waiting for that. And I effortlessly knocked his sword from his hand.

Just as I was going to command him to order a surrender, Ithar joined our fray. As he attacked, Gallun reached down for his sword. I was now in a dire situation. While I would be able to defeat Gallun, facing both together was a daunting task.

Ithar sent a barrage of blows at me, which I barely managed to fend off. When my defense held, Ithar backed off for a moment to catch his breath. Clearly, he had spent himself trying to overwhelm me, and now he had to recover. That was fortunate, as for the moment, I only had to deal with Gallun.

"Traitorous piece of filth," he hissed while renewing his own assault. I parried each of his blows, but I could not find an opening to strike. Gallun glanced at his companion and took a step back. I could see that he was waiting for Ithar to ready himself. When both men were prepared, they pounced. As they advanced, I dove to the ground, rolled, and slashed my sword upwards. It caught Gallun in the stomach, and I felt it cut through skin down to his groin. He collapsed in a heap as I jumped up. Ithar turned to me, ready to strike, but before he could, I knocked his sword from his hand. As he scrambled, I spun him around with my blade against his neck.

"Order your men to stand down," I commanded. Being that Ithar was a mercenary, he owed no loyalty to Mephosh outside of fulfilling his mission. If they were clearly defeated, he would have no qualms with walking away.

With his life hanging in the balance, Ithar called for his men to surrender. He had no power over the soldiers from Mephosh, but they would not continue the conflict with the mercenaries leaving.

As all our foes began to surrender, I called for our men to sheath their weapons. Though I did not have the authority to do so, the surviving warriors followed my command. "Take all their weapons and send them back to their homes. Once they are on their way, set fire to whatever of the siege engines we cannot take with us."

I pushed Ithar away, then dropped to my knees beside my friend. Gallun stared up at me. I saw his entrails spilling from the wound. His eyes were glossy, but they remained focused on me. His mouth moved, trying to form words, but the only thing that emerged was blood.

"I'm sorry, my friend," I managed to say as tears rolled down my cheeks. My blood-soaked hand grasped his as I continued. "You don't know how sorry I am."

His mouth shook a bit, and he managed to say, "Why?"

"I wish I could explain it to you. I wish we had the time for you to hear all of what I experienced. I was released from the lies of my life."

His grip on my hand weakened. His eyes wandered across my face as they tried to refocus. "Me?" he gurgled.

I was not sure what he meant. Was he asking about himself, that he too had lived a lie, or was he asking if I rejected him, my closest friend? I struggled with the words to say as his life drained away. "You are my brother, and I love you as such," and I gently squeezed his hand to emphasize the point. "We were both deceived. The gods are a lie."

A smile formed on his face as his head turned to the side. His eyes stayed open as the last of his life drained onto the ground. I could not control my sobs as I stood. What did that smile mean? Had he acknowledged the love between us in his final moment, or was it simply a cruel jest brought on by his death? I would never know.

The light was almost completely gone, but the blaze starting on a few of the siege towers made it a bit easier to see. "The priest rejects his gods and kills his friend. This is not an outcome I never could have foreseen." I had not realized that Ithar remained where I had left him.

I continued to stare down at Gallun for a few more moments before turning my attention to the mercenary leader. "As I spared your life, I ask only one thing of you. I want you to return to Mephosh and tell Lynna what you saw here. Tell her that I live, and that the gods are a lie. All the northern kingdoms are allied in this regard. Su'Meeryn is now free with a new king and queen, and Mephosh should not consider attacking again. We just want to live in peace."

"You priests are not at all what I had expected. I will do as you ask, but I don't know what you hope to accomplish."

"I don't expect that Lynna will see the truth, but I must try. I will never be able to return to my home and speak with her."

"No, that much is certain."

"Tell her that the creator restored my sight and ended the drought," I said, almost pleading. "What have the gods ever done for anyone?"

Ithar snorted at my words. "I care not for either. I am a practical man, Sul, and my mercenary honor holds me to your request. But after what you have done here, the queen's ears will be deaf to your words."

"I'm sure you are correct, but tell her anyway. Maybe someday she will come to understand."

"You do seem to be a different man from when we last met. But do you really believe all you are saying?"

"I don't merely believe it. I experienced it."

"Hmm," he replied. "I've never been a contemplative man, but perhaps I will ponder your words on the journey back to Mephosh."

"I doubt it, but I do hope so," I said.

"What else will I have to do?" he replied with a chuckle as he walked off.

With that distraction gone, my attention returned to Gallun. What had become of me? I thought of Teyon, the former king of Su'Meeryn, dead at my hands. I thought of all those I had beaten, of Kieran and Wander, two I now called friends. The worshipers I had slaughtered, the soldiers and mercenaries. Now I had killed my best friend.

As I continued to gaze at my friend's body, all my pain returned. My shoulder throbbed, and my calf burned. My lungs hurt so bad I could hardly take a breath. I realized that I was still holding the sword that had ended Gallun's life, and I let it fall from my fingers. Jaleph was now king of Su'Meeryn, and the kingdom was safe from Mephosh. Any trace of the gods in Su'Meeryn would be eradicated. We had won, and I vowed never to grasp a weapon again.

With my blade lying next to him, my eyes remained transfixed on the body of my friend. It amazed me how the two of us, who had been brought up together, studied together, and trained together, could end up so differently.

My tears flowed freely as I again dropped to the ground and reached out for his lifeless hand. It still felt a bit warm. Letting it go, I looked around as a few more of the towers now burned, allowing me to see forms milling about. The light from the fires reflected off the blood-soaked field in a crimson hue. The survivors walked amongst the bodies, searching for signs of life.

Everywhere I looked, I saw filth. No one had escaped unblemished. I do not know if it was a trick of the light, but one figure seemed to stand out. I thought I saw a slight man dressed in a bright white cloak walking along the outskirts of the scene. Certainly, no one could have come out so unscathed from the combat. More movement obscured my view, and then the vision was gone. It was replaced by Jaleph, Kieran, and Wander, who were approaching me.

"There he is!" Kieran called out as they rushed over.

When the three of them surrounded me, I felt Wander's huge hands pull me to my feet. His dark face was camouflaged against the night sky, but in the firelight, his white teeth glistened within his warm smile.

"I saw all of it," Jaleph said. "I watched you fight from our vantage point. I've never seen anything like it. You single-handedly turned the tide of the battle." His joy burst forth, then his expression turned to one of confusion. He could not understand why I was not celebrating.

"Oh my," Kieran said quietly once she recognized the body at our feet. Her eyes softened, and even in the dim light, I saw them turning red. Those kind eyes drifted away from Gallun and back to me. "You?" was all she could say, but the question was unnecessary. She knew I was the one responsible for my friend's death.

"Yes," was my only reply. I wanted to tell them to make sure they gave Gallun a proper burial, but I knew Kieran would see to it. I needed to get away from that place. I would never forget this moment, but I could no longer stand beside body of the last man that I had slain.

As I started to walk away, I stumbled from the pain in my calf and fell against Wander's large frame. Rather than push myself away, I allowed my body to lean against his. Without realizing what I was doing, my arms wrapped around him as my sobs returned. He engulfed me in his grip as my tears fell.

I was vaguely aware of hands probing my legs, and then I felt a bandage being wrapped around my wounded calf. The queen had obviously noticed my stumble and found the wound.

How long we remained there, I know not. Eventually, Jaleph ordered us to start the trek north. It was completely dark now, but he wanted us to get away from this grisly scene before we camped for the night.

We had lost many of the horses in the battle, either killed or ran off, so the journey back would be slow. With the number of wounded and with so few horses left, Jaleph had decided that we could not bring any of the siege engines with us. We left all of them ablaze as we made our way north. Jaleph did not know when troops might be able to return to retrieve them, and nobody wanted to risk them falling back in Lynna's hands.

Despite my protests, I had been offered a horse as one of the wounded. But after trying to walk for a few steps, I knew I would never be able to make it back to Su'Meeryn on foot. So I reluctantly agreed, and I was thankful once I was off my feet.

We only traveled for perhaps an hour until Jaleph called a halt for the night. As sentries were stationed, I was glad that soon I would be able to sleep. At least then, I would no longer be thinking of Gallun.

While I stretched out on the ground, Pytr came up to me. I was told that he had survived, but this was the first time I had seen him since the battle had ended. "I'm glad you are alive," I said.

"As am I of you," he responded as he sat next to me. "I heard of what you did. Many are talking about it. They say nobody has seen a warrior fight as you did today. The battle appeared to be turning against us until then. Some are saying it was magical."

"Magic had nothing to do with it, but I did seem to have received some assistance. I wish I could explain it."

"No need," he replied. "I also heard about your friend. That is an outcome I pray that I never have to experience."

I felt numb at his words, but then my shoulder throbbed again. In a way, I guess it was fitting that I was the one who had killed Gallun. One more misery to be added to all the others. I thought of Juna and the children, the pleasant times spent in their home, gambling and sharing meals. All the banter and the wine. They would certainly hear that I was the one who had killed him. How would they handle that? Of course, that really was not a mystery. They would hate me as much as he did at the end, more so. They would hate me as much as I hated myself. After all I had done, I deserved this sorrow too.

"You have been given a difficult task to bear, Sul. Don't let it overwhelm you."

"What do you mean by that?"

"Just what I said. I can't imagine all the guilt you feel."

"Who could?" I asked.

Pytr offered a friendly laugh. "I don't suppose anyone could, which I suppose puts you in a unique position."

"If it was all the same, I'd rather not be in this position."

"No, I suppose not. But we can't choose the hardships that are placed on us."

"You are correct there," I replied, "but we are responsible for some."

"True," Pytr said. "Once we arrive back in Su'Meeryn, my men and I will stay for a bit to rest. I look forward to talking with you further."

"I would like that." I gazed at the man who looked so different from when we first met. All the pomp was gone, and I saw nothing but an exhausted warrior. He had managed to wipe away some of the blood, but he was a mess, as were the rest of us. "If you will excuse me," I continued. "I'm still in a bit of pain, and I hope that I will be able to get some sleep."

"Of course. We will talk again."

With Pytr gone, I wrapped my arm over my eyes, wondering if sleep would come. Thankfully, my exhaustion quickly overwhelmed me, and all the pain and guilt dissolved away.

Chapter 20

I SAT IN MY ROOM AND CHANGED THE DRESSING on my leg. We had arrived back at Su'Meeryn late the night before, greeted by much fanfare, but I had retired immediately to my room. I was in too much pain and did not feel like celebrating; the vision of Gallun's lifeless body haunted me. The morning came far too early, and I did not enjoy waking up. All consciousness did was remind me of my pain.

Once I had dressed, I walked to the door. The calf ached a bit, but that pain was subsiding quickly. Unfortunately, I could not say the same regarding my arm. If anything, the shoulder felt worse. I opened the door to head down for breakfast to find Wander and the queen about to knock.

"Hello," I said, surprised to see them this early.

"Ah, good," Wander replied. "We hoped to find you before you headed down. May we enter?"

"Of course," I answered as I turned to allow them in.

Kieran sat on my single chair, and Wander motioned at the bed. "You need to sit more than me," he said.

"Thank you," I responded as I went back to the bed.

Once I was situated, Wander continued. "I can't imagine what you are going through. I know how much you love our home and the queen. That is not to even mention Gallun. How are you holding up?"

I stared silently at the large man. I wanted to bark at him, but words failed me. What did he expect me to say? It was a ridiculous question. But I would never be able to raise my voice to this man. His scars remained visible, a constant reminder of my former self. "I'm miserable," I replied honestly.

"We are sorry that we've added more burdens to you," Kieran stated.

"Please don't apologize to me; that is the last thing I want to hear. You all deserve my complete loyalty for all you have done for me."

"Nonetheless, it was never our intention."

"I thank you for your kindness. If it weren't for the two of you, I would have died in my ignorance."

"Yes, but now that the turmoil is behind us, we need to think about what is next for you," Wander said.

"I don't know," I responded. "All I know is that I will never kill again. My days of combat are behind me."

"That is understandable," Wander continued, "but you still have much you can offer. No priest of your stature has ever rejected the gods, at least not that I know of. You could be of great service to the creator."

I grunted in disapproval at his words. I knew not what the future would offer me, but I did not feel like I could be of further service. What value could I possibly offer anyone?

"At some point, you are going to have to forgive yourself," Kieran said. Before I could interject, she continued. "We all know what you have done. Your past will never be erased, but you cannot wallow in it. What you did to us and to many in the kingdom stemmed from your ignorance, the lie that raised you. No, that is not an excuse. You still made your choices, and you will live with the consequences. You killed your closest friend, and you will be in pain for the rest of your life. But you will need to move on at some point."

I considered her words. Was there truth there? If so, I did not see it. How could I move on from my sins? "I will consider what you say." I stood, looked down at her, and added, "Majesty," and she smiled affectionally at the title.

"Let us break our fast together," Wander offered as we exited the room.

As we started down the hall, we heard a commotion from behind. Four guards hurried down the hall with swords out. They stopped when they reached us and appeared a bit flustered when they spotted their new queen. "What is the meaning of this?" Kieran asked angrily.

The first man sheathed his sword and looked worriedly at her. "I apologize, my queen, but we have orders to arrest Sul."

"Orders… arrest… Sul," she stammered. "Orders from whom?"

"King Jaleph."

"Jaleph ordered this?" Wander asked angrily.

The soldier glanced at Wander, obviously not recognizing him as a man of importance in the kingdom. He turned back to Kieran, and she simply stared back at him. "Yes, the king commanded that he be taken to the dungeons."

"We shall see about that," Kieran said forcefully. "You all wait here."

She spun to leave when I stopped her. "Please don't. I will go with them."

The queen turned back to me with a mix of anger and sadness in her beautiful eyes. "I will get to the bottom of this."

"That's okay," I said as I followed the guards toward the dungeons.

***

My cell was dark and cold. When my eyes adjusted, I realized that I had a companion with me. As the individual's features took form, I heard a familiar chuckle. "Well, well, the mighty Sul finds himself in my predicament."

"Oziah, I see that you are still imprisoned."

"Not for long," he replied stoically. "They tell me I am to be crucified today."

A gasp escaped my lips at his comment. It was a difficult revelation that I would be losing another friend. I suppose it had been unlikely that Su'Meeryn would ever free the man who had conquered their castle and had been established by Lynna as her regent of the city. But execution? And in such a vile manner?

"I am truly sorry to hear that," I responded.

"At least I know you will be following me."

I felt a twinge in my shoulder as I sat on the damp floor. "I don't know what is to become of me."

"They don't throw you in prison to give you an award."

"That is true." I wanted to tell him of the battle in the plains and how I had been instrumental in stopping Mephosh's advance. But that raised too many memories I did not want to relive. And Oziah would probably have questions that I did not want to answer.

"So your past has finally caught up with you. You didn't think these heretics would forgive you and let you live among them, did you?"

His question fell upon me like Su'Meeryn's crumbling wall when we had first conquered the kingdom. Had I been living in a delusion? What had I expected to happen? "I didn't think anything. I did what I felt I needed to do."

"Fight against your own people?"

I pondered my response for a moment. How could I make him understand? "I know you won't believe me, but what I did was for the good of Su'Meeryn and Mephosh. The gods are a lie, Oziah. The land needs to be free of the pagan religion. Don't you see? It's the belief in the gods that has brought on all this suffering. Paganism made us believe that we were better than those we call heretics. Paganism made me the man I was: a man who killed with no remorse. How can you not see that?"

Oziah's reply surprised me. "Perhaps you're right." His voice was resigned and stoic. "The gods never did anything for me, and look where I'm at."

I crossed the cell to sit next to my friend. It was strange to think that this man, whom I had known for most of my life, was awaiting his execution, and was it because of me? Would I be the cause of his death too? I sighed heavily as I tried to explain myself. I told him about my killing of Teyon and the blow from Jaleph that almost took my life. I recounted the mercy shown me by Wander and Kieran. Then I described how my vision was restored at the moment the rains began to fall.

"There is more going on here than you know, Oziah." I then described my transformation during the last two battles. That was not something that could be explained away.

We continued to talk as the light from the small window began to fade. As the day approached its end, Oziah's words started to become frantic. I sensed his fear growing as we both knew what awaited him. A rattling at the door brought our conversation to an abrupt end. As the door opened, I did not know how Oziah would respond. The guards stood braced, with their weapons drawn, awaiting a violent reaction. But Oziah slowly and calmly stood. "Let's get this over with," he said as he walked toward them. Before they left the cell, he turned back to me. "I will think on what you said, Sul, while I wait for my death."

As the door was closing behind him, all I could say was, "I will pray for you, my friend." And that was what I did all the remainder of the night.

***

The next morning, my door opened, rousing me from my sleep. The queen and Wander entered and instructed the guards, who looked extremely uncomfortable, to stay on the other side of the wall.

"It is good to see you two," I said. I wanted to ask about Oziah, but I decided against it. What could they tell me that I did not know? And I really had no desire to hear any details.

"You should know that this was not Jaleph's decision," stated Kieran. "The nobles demanded that you be arrested and executed."

"I see."

"Know that I argued against this," Wander said. "The king and I both told them of your deeds, how you saved Jaleph, and that we might not have been victorious on the plains if not for you. They understand, but they are not willing to forgive you for the past atrocities."

"Understandable," was all I said. What more was there for me to say?

"Please understand, we did all we could," Kieran continued in a pleading tone. "Jaleph has been king for only a short time. They threatened to reverse the coronation if he did not comply. There is nothing we can do to save you."

A smile grew on my face at her comment. "You both did already. I have been saved, and it was because of you. I'm resigned to my fate, whatever that might be. I stood and approached them. I gently raised my hand to Kieran's face; she did not flinch or back away. Slowly, my finger traced along her scar, then I felt around her disfigured ear. Tears started to flow down her cheeks as she took hold of my hand.

"It is very bittersweet," said Wander. "I was right about you. We would not be in the position that we are now if it wasn't for you. I hate to see it end this way. You are not the man you once were. Know this: you have been of great service to the creator."

"What more could I ask for?"

The pair stayed for a long while. We chatted about other things. Kieran described how strange it felt to be a queen and all the adjustments she would need to make. Wander said that he would remain in Su'Meeryn to help Jaleph establish the proper temples and work to train new clerics. I asked about Mephosh and how Su'Meeryn would interact with their neighbor. None of that had been decided. Nobody wanted more hostilities, but a friendly relationship would not be possible while Lynna remained on the throne. Eventually, they excused themselves and told me they would return as often as possible. I thanked them, and when they left, I started to pray. My petitions were for my homeland and Lynna's enlightenment.

Chapter 21

A GOOD-HEARTED LAUGH BURST FROM MY MOUTH as Pytr entered my cell the next day; I saw no reason to hide it. He was wearing the most outlandish outfit I had yet seen him in, and of course, his face was shaved and sported elaborate cosmetics. Green trousers sat above orange boots, and a pink shirt shone under a black and blue jacket. Atop his head was a brown cap with one yellow feather jutting at an angle. He turned from side to side to display his attire. "Do you like it?"

I laughed again. "Where did you find such things?"

"It was not easy, let me tell you. I'm still looking for the perfect pair of earrings."

"Well, I wish you success with your mission."

He chuckled for a moment, but the twinkle in his eyes quickly darkened. "I will be returning home today, and I had to make sure I saw you before then."

"I appreciate that."

He removed his ridiculous hat to scratch the top of his head. "It is sad that you will not be able to visit me in Amyon. I was looking forward to conversing more with you, and I thought I would have been able to take you on a hunt or two."

"I would have enjoyed that. At least, I think I would have. As a priest, I never hunted."

"That is a shame. Few things bring me as much happiness as being out in the wilderness and acquiring my own meal."

"I will take your word regarding the matter, but it does sound pleasing."

Pytr's sad expression morphed into one of confusion. "Forgive me if I'm overreaching, Sul, but you seem resigned to your fate. It's almost like you are looking forward to it."

"Let me assure you that that is not the case. I would prefer to live, but I understand the nobles' decision."

"Nobles," Pytr spat. "I've never had much use for them. They care for nothing but their own desires. They can't see past their self-interests."

"Of course I would rather live," I explained, "but our choices have consequences. Even if those choices were made from a faulty perspective."

Pytr placed the hat back on his head. "That is true, but these nobles would no longer be nobles if it wasn't for you."

"That might be so, but I have brought this fate upon myself."

"Well my friend," Pytr said, sighing deeply. "I unfortunately must be on my way. I need to get the remainder of my warriors back to Amyon. I deeply regret that this is the last time I will see you. I have greatly enjoyed our talks."

I stood and crossed the small distance to that preposterous yet endearing man. "As have I." He reached out his hand, and I grasped it warmly. "It is my honor to know you," I said. "I too regret that we will have no further time together."

Pytr knocked on the door for the guard to release him. He removed his hat again, bowed to me, then offered a wink. A broad smile crossed his face as I laughed at the gesture, then he exited the cell. The door closed behind him, and I was left alone.

***

"I've been wanting to see you, but I was trying to find the appropriate time," Jaleph said as he stood by the wall, looking across the cell at me.

"I understand," I replied. "Kieran has been here often. She is a remarkable woman."

"Yes, she is."

"And Wander has come with her at times," I added.

"I know you've been told this isn't my decision, but I wanted to reaffirm that. My reign as king is currently precarious. If the nobles had me removed, they would install another, and your fate would be the same. This is the only demand they have of me. They want you to pay for your crimes."

"I can't fault them for that decision. They know all I've done."

"You seem very accepting of this," Jaleph pointed out.

"I am."

"As you know, I was initially against saving your life. I watched you kill Teyon, as well as the countless other innocents. I saw it all," the king said as his eyes drifted to his missing arm.

"You don't need to remind me. I am never separated from my memories. Every twinge of pain in my shoulder is a reminder of all that I did."

Jaleph sighed, and I noticed a trace of his own discomfort flutter across his face. "It's hard for me to forget too. I lost my arm, and I still have my own pain. But I must admit that Wander was correct in saving you. You have served us all well, and I never saw anyone fight like you did."

"I can't take credit for that. I'm still not sure what overcame me. What you witnessed did not come from me."

"Regardless of how it happened, it was you that saved my life and brought us victory against Mephosh. We owe you a debt."

Those words were hard for me to accept, but I did not want to profess false modesty. I was well aware of all that I had done and all that I had accomplished. But did those heroic deeds erase all my transgression? And I was still haunted by visions of Gallun's corpse.

"For days, I have petitioned for your pardon, but they refused. The only consolation they gave was that you will not be crucified like Oziah. Your execution will be as quick and painless as possible."

"That is more than I deserve."

"They did say you could beg for your life, but I would advise against it. They are not going to relent, and they would only use that to humiliate you."

Beg for my life? After all the death I had caused, pleading for clemency was the last thing I would do. "I'm sure you are right."

"In a way, this might be the most merciful outcome for you, Sul. You have been enlightened, and I know how your past plagues you. This will free you from your misery. But I don't want you to die."

His words rang true, and they were exactly how I felt. I did not want to die, but my memories were more of a distress to me than the throbbing in my arm.

"I need to depart, but before I leave, I want you to know, Sul, that I forgive you. This was not an easy position for me to come to, but it is true. Yes, you believed a lie, but that is not justification for all those atrocities. You made your choices, hence your forthcoming execution. But I see the man that you are now. It is not just because of your exploits on the battlefield. I see the regret and shame in your eyes. It did take me a while, as I am a stubborn man, but I forgive you."

My throat caught as I managed to thank him. He looked at me for another moment, then left the cell. As the cell door closed behind the king, my tears began to flow. They ran down my face like the time I had killed my best friend. I fell on the floor and continued to sob, but my tears were different this time. Yes, I still felt my guilt. I had not forgotten my victims, but I now felt some semblance of peace creeping into my soul. My actions could not be erased, and I would suffer the consequence of those. But if Jaleph, of all people, could forgive me, perhaps absolution was possible. For the first time, I actually felt I was truly forgiven.

Epilogue

WHEN I HAD FINALLY FINISHED MY STORY, the inquisitor dropped his parchment, and silence hung over the cell like an early morning fog. “That is quite a tale,” he finally said.

“I’m not sure that is how I would characterize it,” I replied.

He gathered up his pages as he stood. “You still have one last opportunity to beg for your life, but after hearing your story, I’m sure you won’t.”

“You are correct.”

Just before he left my cell, he turned back to me. “Oh, I thought you should know. I was told that before Oziah died, he renounced the gods and begged to be forgiven.”

My face brightened at those words. “That is good to hear.”

“Sul, I’m glad I was the one ordered to attend to you. I will make sure that your story is remembered and passed on to the other kingdoms.”

“Thank you. I know it is unlikely, but please try to send a copy to Mephosh. I’m certain I am hated there, but I would like the people to understand what I did.”

“I know Mephosh has some believers. We will make every effort that copies of this make their way to them.”

“Thank you again.” He nodded as he opened the door. “When will it happen?” I asked.

“They say tomorrow. Jaleph has still been trying to get them to rescind their demand, but he has been unsuccessful.”

“I would assume that to be the case,” I commented.

“Goodbye, Sul. I will admit, before I met you, I was eager to see you die. But know this. I will take no pleasure in your execution.”

There was nothing left to say to the man. He hesitated for a brief moment, waiting for a further response, but when I remained silent, he left the room. And I was alone.

A sense of calm overcame me. So tomorrow was the day. I did not look forward to it, but I did not dread it, either. I thought of Gallun, and Oziah, and Teyon. I thought of the worshipers in Su'Meeryn. As all those rolled through my mind, the pain in my shoulder increased, but I welcomed it.

My thoughts turned to Kieran, Wander, and Jaleph. So much death and so much wrong, but the grace and forgiveness that I had been granted overwhelmed me.

I stood up and looked out the small window. The sun was high in the sky, and I felt a bit of warmth against my face. The sky was a crisp blue, and I saw traces of a few billowing clouds. It was nice to have a vision of beauty before experiencing my ultimate fate.

There was a knock at my door, and it opened again. A guard dropped a plate of food and a large mug of cool water. Final meal, I thought. I sat on the ground beside the tray and found a small, cooked bird and a handful of carrots, along with a few pieces of bread. The food supplies in Su'Meeryn were still low, so I figured Jaleph or Kieran must have seen to this generous delivery.

After I finished the food, I turned my attention to the mug. I took a sip of the water; it refreshed me as it traveled down my throat. I thought of the drought that had lasted so long, then I thought of that moment when my vision had been restored, and the rains finally came. I took another drink and savored the fresh liquid.

Once the mug was empty, I stood and returned to the small window. My arm still hurt, but I took some consolation that tomorrow the pain would be gone. I relished the sliver of sunlight that touched my skin.

I inhaled deeply then heard a commotion in the courtyard on the other side of the dungeon. Cries sounded, and it seemed that they were directed against each other. Over the tumult, I heard one voice shouting above the others for quiet. Eventually, the cacophony subsided.

"I have as much reason as any to see him dead." I recognized the voice of Jaleph. "My arm is gone, and look at my wife's face. I watched him slaughter our clerics, and I saw him kill my friend Teyon, but trust me, he has suffered greatly from his deeds."

"Not enough," a solitary voice shouted back.

"You made me your king for a reason. Have faith in me regarding this matter."

"We have been over this many times," the same man responded. "He has to pay for his crimes, Jaleph."

"I never said he didn't. We can debate whether he has suffered enough, but we should not kill him."

"How much longer do we have to debate this? All are aware of his deeds since renouncing the gods; however, those do not erase his past. We offered mercy by approving a quick death. What about consequences?" The crowd began to murmur again, but they quieted when I heard Wander call for silence.

"I'm not calling for a full pardon," the king continued, "but agree with me on this, stay the execution." I heard a pleading tone in his words.

There was a long pause, and I was surprised that the silence remained. Eventually, the man continued, "Very well, Jaleph. In deference to you, the nobles will meet again tonight. We will let you know our decision in the morning."

"Thank you all. Your king and queen appreciate your decision," I heard Kieran respond as the crowd began to disperse.

The thought of my life possibly being spared seemed to make the light from the window a bit brighter and warmer. I offered a slight smile to the small amount of visible sky. As I sat back down, I felt that all too familiar twinge in my shoulder, but even that pain seemed to decrease.

I did not know what the morning would bring, but in a sense, the nobles' ultimate decision did not matter. I knew that I was the most wicked of all sinners, but I was also the most blessed. Somehow, I had been granted absolution.

I was ready to meet my fate.

www.ingramcontent.com/pod-product-compliance
Lightning Source LLC
LaVergne TN
LVHW020633100826
845148LV00012B/2167

9781638681205